BELOW DECK BILLIONAIRE

AMY ANDREWS

Boldwood

First published in Great Britain in 2025 by Boldwood Books Ltd.

Copyright © Amy Andrews, 2025

Cover Design by Colin Thomas

Cover Images: Colin Thomas

Every effort has been made to obtain the necessary permissions with reference to copyright material, both illustrative and quoted. We apologise for any omissions in this respect and will be pleased to make the appropriate acknowledgements in any future edition.

A CIP catalogue record for this book is available from the British Library.

Paperback ISBN 978-1-83617-972-6

Large Print ISBN 978-1-83617-973-3

Hardback ISBN 978-1-83617-971-9

Ebook ISBN 978-1-83617-974-0

Kindle ISBN 978-1-83617-975-7

Audio CD ISBN 978-1-83617-966-5

MP3 CD ISBN 978-1-83617-967-2

Digital audio download ISBN 978-1-83617-968-9

This book is printed on certified sustainable paper. Boldwood Books is dedicated to putting sustainability at the heart of our business. For more information please visit https://www.boldwoodbooks.com/about-us/sustainability/

Boldwood Books Ltd, 23 Bowerdean Street, London, SW6 3TN

www.boldwoodbooks.com

To Mykonos – you have my whole heart.

1

Few people in this world would dare give Theodorus Callisthenes – heir to Ōceanós, a multi-billion-dollar Greek cruise ship company – a right royal bollocking. After all, his name meant 'gift from God.'

Unfortunately, his brother hadn't got the memo.

'What. The. Fuck.' Aristotle stormed into his office, eyes black as thunder, brandishing what seemed to be a newspaper.

Theo wasn't alarmed. In fact, quite the opposite. It was good to see some spark and fire in Ari after all those bleak years triggered by his first wife's death. Since meeting Kelsey, and marrying her three months ago, his younger brother had come back to them. The Callisthenes family had a lot to thank the ex-cocktail waitress for and Theo would weather whatever foul mood Ari threw at him to have his brother happy again. Living again.

A woman he loved and a baby on the way.

'I've just been on the phone to Dimitri Kouris who is backing out of the deal we've spent three months negotiating and the last three weeks putting the finer touches on, because of this.'

Ari slapped exhibit A on the desk, which turned out to be a trashy but popular tabloid rag. With Theo – above and below the centre fold – on the front page. It was a little grainy but for sure it was him, taken through partially open French doors, large as life, bare-ass naked, his modesty blurred out, indulging in a three-way embrace with two women, appropriate bits of them blurred but also very obviously naked.

Well... fuck.

Theo glanced at the picture dispassionately. Once upon a time the memory would have made him smile, but all he remembered now was how his heart hadn't really been in the experience. Had he performed adequately? Yes. Had they gone away happy the morning after? Yes. Had it helped him to stop thinking about her? About Tiffany?

No. It had not.

'The online pictures are even worse.'

Theo could only imagine. 'What can I say?' Theo shrugged. 'Women like me.'

His brother was clearly not in the mood for flippancy. 'Three months,' Ari roared, 'down the drain because you can't keep your cock zipped.'

The rather inappropriate urge to laugh took hold at the role reversal that was now playing out. Not that long ago it had been him yelling at his brother to get a life. Insisting he leave his den of grief and sending him undercover onto the *Hellenic Spirit* with strict orders to not only investigate what was going wrong with the cruise ship but to also have some goddamn fun for a change.

But laughter right now would be a bigger transgression than flippancy.

'What I do in my private time is none of Dimitri's or anyone else's business.'

'But it's not private, is it?' Ari hissed, ramming his index finger into that blurred-out segment of Theo's anatomy. 'It's all over the tabloids!'

'That's hardly my fault.'

Why was he responsible because some pap with a zoom lens as big as the Acropolis had illegally invaded his privacy, catching him and two very lovely and very anonymous women in flagrante inside a hotel room in what was an entirely consensual tryst?

'Oh, don't be so fucking naive,' Ari snapped. 'You're a rich, Greek playboy that the tabloids love to exploit for clicks. Shut your goddamn doors.'

Calmly folding the paper, Theo dumped it in the bin under his desk before rising from his chair and crossing to the expansive glass panelling that afforded him a bird's-eye view across the Athens skyline. The clutter of buildings both new and ancient sat cheek by jowl, dominated by the rise of the Acropolis and the crumbled majesty of the Parthenon sitting atop the rocky outcrop. In the distance he could see the frenetic shipping activity at Piraeus and the sparkling water of the Aegean beyond.

From his luxuriously appointed penthouse office suite, he felt like a god, surveying the Callisthenes empire. Like Zeus staring down from Mount Olympus. And it never failed to swell his chest with pride in his family and love for his country.

But lately... now? He just felt restless. And unfocused. Like there was more to life than a shipping empire and this million-dollar view.

Sliding in beside him, Ari folded his arms and also stared out the window. He didn't say anything for long moments, as transfixed as Theo as they stood side by side in brotherly solidarity. They spent a lot of time doing this, just standing here admiring the view together recognising in silence how blessed they'd been in life.

The Callisthenes family had come a long way from the moment their *pappou* had taken his *pappou*'s struggling tender business – which he'd traded for several small fishing boats at the age of twenty – to an international juggernaut.

'You know as well as I do,' Ari said eventually, his tone more conciliatory, addressing the window, not Theo, 'how eye-wateringly conservative Dimitri is. And as long-term friends of Marco Konstantinides, he already wasn't your biggest fan.'

Konstantinides. The name jabbed the spot inside that no amount of sexual shenanigans or three-way trysts could erase. He was thirty-five years old and still felt the guilt and shame of what had happened when he was eighteen. Angelika Konstantinides had well and truly moved on, finding happiness with a family of her own, but many, it seemed, had not.

'What's the old man playing at?' Theo didn't address his brother, either. 'We don't need him. He needs us. He would cut off his nose to spite his face?'

'Probably. Yes. He's as proud as he is conservative.'

'We're trying to throw him a lifeline.'

Dimitri, an old friend of Yanis Callisthenes – Theo and Ari's grandfather – ran a successful but comparatively small charter business. Or he had anyway. It was now seriously on the rocks and taking on water. It was only a matter of time before it went under. And the old curmudgeon seemed determined to go down with it.

But what of the fate of his almost three hundred employees? Ōceanós could easily absorb the Kouris company and give them the lifeline they desperately needed.

'I wouldn't put it past him to go with one of our competitors.'

Frustration boiled in Theo's gut. 'But they'll break his company up and sell it off bit by bit. We'll keep it intact and running and get it turning a profit again. He knows this.'

Damn it, if it were up to Theo he'd cut the old fool loose. Let him fuck around and find out just how much worse off his company would be if one of the sharks ominously circling was to swallow it whole. Theo Callisthenes would look like a goddamn angel by the time the snack-sized Kouris empire had been devoured.

But they'd promised their grandfather they would get this done. And as Ari kept reminding him – it made good business sense.

'He's a Greek man of a certain age, which means he's bull-headed and used to having things go his way. This whole experience had humbled him and he's angry and wounded and looking for any excuse to not take charity from one of his oldest friends.'

'Charity?' Theo snorted. 'The price he's asking for that lemon is extortionate.'

Ari fell silent, obviously not, as the CFO, prepared to dispute Theo's statement even though he knew it to be right and they both stared at the view for long moments.

'What's up with you?' Ari asked, finally interrupting the silence.

Feeling his brother's gaze on his profile, Theo muttered dismissively, 'I'm fine.' Because if he knew the answer to that he'd be doing something about it. None of the usual things – partying, sailing and polo – were working any more.

'No, you're not. You've been acting like the world's supply of available women is about to run out and you're trying to get to every single one of them. I mean... you've always been ridiculously horny, but this is extra even for you. You're out of control.'

Theo clenched his jaw. His brother's summary hit a little too close to the bone. 'I'm not,' he ground out, tension creeping into his neck and shoulders. After fucking up badly when he was younger, Theo maintained ruthless control over his sex life.

One and done.

'Yes. You are. It's like you're on goddamn heat or something. What happened?'

'Nothing happened.' *Do not think about Tiffany. Do. Not.* 'You're just jealous because you'll only ever sleep with the one woman for the rest of your days.'

Instead of feeling chastised or insulted, Ari threw his head back and laughed like it was the dumbest comeback he'd ever heard. 'Theo, Theo, Theo.' Ari clapped him on the shoulder. 'One day you're going to learn that there is something better than sex.'

'Let me guess.' Theo held the back of his palm to his forehead for dramatic effect as he slipped his hand across his heart. 'Stroking the belly of your pregnant wife?'

That was not for Theo. He'd taken care of that potential a long time ago, getting a vasectomy at the age of twenty-two.

'Close.' Ari grinned. 'Sex with a woman you love.'

Theo rolled his eyes. His brother always had been a one-woman guy. Unlike himself, who'd been team one-night stand ever since the fiasco with Angelika. 'Now you sound like Pappou.'

Their grandparents had been married for over sixty years and were still madly in love. Openly affectionate and utterly content in each other's company, they extolled the virtues of love, marriage and monogamy with all the zeal of cult members. His parents had also sipped the Kool-Aid.

Ari grinned. 'That's because he knows what he's talking about.'

Sex with love. Something Theo had avoided at all costs and

yet, after keeping her firmly out of his brain for this conversation, he was suddenly thinking about Tiffany.

Again.

Tiffany, who he hadn't had to have *the conversation* with because she hadn't been there the next morning when he'd woken. Tiffany, who hadn't returned his messages or even, apparently, asked after him. Tiffany, who'd returned his flowers.

Which was perfectly fine. Just the way he liked it. Not having to spell it out in an excruciating conversation he'd had once too often? Bonus.

Except for this damn restlessness.

Glancing at his brother, he asked, 'Can you get Dimitri back to the table?'

Returning his gaze, Ari shook his head slowly. 'I don't think so.'

Hmph. That was not an acceptable answer. He'd rather face the wrath of his brother than the disappointment of his grandfather. 'Oh, come on. Your negotiation skills are second to none.'

Theo was the risk taker, the CEO with wile and cunning and an eye for identifying the deals that would keep the company agile and growing both within the shipping industry and beyond. Ari negotiated the deals. That was the way they worked and as a team, they were formidable.

'Yeah, well, currently they're second to you being able to keep your dick in your pants so I don't see him coming back anytime soon.'

Theo snorted. 'You think I can't go without sex?'

Another hearty laugh from his brother, who was clutching his abdomen like the statement was hilarious. When he sobered, he frowned at Theo's unimpressed face. 'Oh.' His brow wrinkled. 'That was a serious question?'

Theo crossed his arms. 'Yes.' *Malakas.*

'Okay... if current hook-up patterns are any indication, the answer is a big hell no.'

His brother's absolute certainty rankled. Theo's hackles rose along with his competitive spirit. 'Wanna bet?' He wasn't some teenager who couldn't control his urges. Sure, he'd let them have free reign but that didn't mean they weren't under his command.

'Definitely.' Ari grinned as he held out his hand. 'I dare you to go without sex for four months.'

'Four months?' Theo's brow dipped. Firstly, ugh. It had been a very long time since he'd gone four days without. Secondly, why four?

'It's going to take me another few months to convince him you're a reformed man. Plus, I do have responsibilities other than trailing after you fixing your fuckups. Like preparing financial statements for the end of tax year, which are due in a few months.'

It was Theo's turn to laugh. He'd forgotten Ari's brain was ruled by the four quarters of the tax season. Once a finance guy, always a finance guy. 'Tell me, do you take your slide rule to bed to impress your wife?'

Wisely, Ari did not take the bait; he just smiled knowingly and kept his hand extended waiting for Theo to shake. 'Too long, huh?'

Theo hesitated. Four months. Approximately one hundred and twenty days. That was a long-ass time to go without the world's greatest recreational activity. Maybe too long?

'Define sex.' Maybe there was some wriggle room?

'You need me to tell you about special cuddles?'

Theo would rather cut off his ears. 'I know you're a boring married guy now but I'm sure you remember there are myriad ways a guy can have sexy fun times with a woman that doesn't involve special cuddles.'

Ari dropped his hand. 'Already working out how to game the system.' He shook his head. 'I would expect nothing less, brother.'

Theo smiled. 'I'm merely seeking to understand the parameters of the dare. Do you mean no sex in the biblical sense or...'

'How about' – Ari ticked each point off his fingers – 'no kissing, no nudity, no penetration.'

Hmph. All the fun things. 'No kissing? Isn't that a bit extreme?'

Ari shrugged. 'It's a gateway thing, you know that.'

'A gateway thing?'

'Name one woman you've kissed – on the mouth – that you haven't had sex with?'

Theo searched his memory banks to dispute Ari's claim. But even a cursory examination told him there was no name to be found. And the fact his brother knew that about him made him extra pissy. 'You know I can do all those things in privacy and you'd never know.'

'Sure.' His brother shot him a sardonic smile. 'But you never do. That's the problem. And if you think I won't know then think again. There's a reason I do the negotiating. I'll know. And besides, I'm calling on your honour as a Callisthenes.'

Goddamn it. Ari had him there. Nothing was more important to a Callisthenes than honour. 'What do I get? If I win the dare?'

'The honour of knowing you won?'

Theo snorted. He hated how well his brother knew him sometimes. Didn't mean he wasn't going to push him for more, though. 'That seems like a terrible deal.'

'Okay then, the knowledge that I was wrong and you were right.'

'And being able to rub it in whenever I want.'

'Naturally,' Ari agreed dryly.

'What about...' Theo made a crude motion with his right hand.

Ari grinned. 'You can beat yourself raw.'

Thank Zeus for small mercies. If Theo agreed to this ridiculous dare, he'd probably end up with RSI in his wrist.

'You can't do it, can you?' Ari said, repeating his taunt as he presented his hand again.

The *I told you so* in his brother's voice rammed a rod of steel up Theo's spine. He was used to taking gambles in business and doing whatever it took to win. He could achieve whatever he set his mind to. And his grandfather needed this done.

Besides, he hadn't been able to fuck his way out of his weird funk. Maybe he could deprive his way out?

He slid his hand into Ari's, and they shook. 'You got a deal.'

2

TWO MONTHS LATER...

Tiffany Wainwright was hard to impress. She grew up on an outback cattle station that covered almost ten thousand square kilometres. Where she came from, they mustered cattle with helicopters. Large saltwater crocs lurked in the river that ran along the western boundary. She'd lost count of the number of snakes she'd encountered.

Once, when she'd been seven, a royal prince had stayed for a week.

And later, when she'd left Australia at the age of eighteen, escaping family drama to go on a grand adventure, she'd hiked to the Mount Everest base camp, danced under the Northern Lights in Iceland and walked the Great Wall of China.

Eight years ago, at the age of twenty, she started working on cruise ships. Huge floating hotels with theatres and casinos that had taken her all around the world. For the last three years she'd worked as a casino croupier onboard the *Hellenic Spirit* where the amount of money that was won and lost every night was eye-watering.

All that was to say that while she might have come from the

middle of nowhere, she hadn't just fallen off the turnip truck. Still, the gleaming superyacht secured to its mooring before her was impressive. Not because of its size or its twenty-million-dollar price tag, but because of what it represented.

Exclusivity.

No four thousand people on this boat, most of whom had saved up their hard-earned cash to afford the extravagance of spending time at sea. No upselling to the high-end drinks package or the most expensive shore excursion option. This was luxury only a select few could afford.

The hull was blindingly white under the intense September sunshine that drenched the island of Hydra in bright golden light. It illuminated the clear water fringing the rocky edges of the harbour wall, bounced off terracotta rooftops and dazzled like diamonds on the sea that deepened beyond the harbour mouth.

Her gaze fell on the loopy calligraphy flowing down the side that confirmed this was, indeed, the *Nerida*. And for the next two months, it was going to be her home.

A flutter of anticipation and excitement winged its way through Tiffany's belly. Or maybe it was nervousness. It was the first time she'd worked on something this small, and she wasn't sure of her role. The agency had said it would be steward work – cleaning, serving, bar work – with occasional croupier duties, which was why, largely, she'd scored the job.

Anyone could be taught to make a bed and fix a margarita, but becoming a professional croupier was a much more specialised area and not something that could be taught overnight. Of course, she'd never done it in such a bespoke environment before, but she was up for the challenge and she'd kick ass doing it because that was what she did.

A girl who'd grown up roping and wrangling cows and

cowboys knew how to work hard and wasn't afraid to get dirty doing it. And besides, she had to because life on a huge cruise ship hadn't been working for her for the last few months.

Too many people. Too little space. Too little privacy. Not enough free time.

None of those things had bothered her before, but they did now. Which was why when her contract came up for renewal a month ago, she'd decided not to re-sign. She hadn't known what she'd wanted but when the agency had come back to her with this job, it had seemed like a good stepping stone to whatever was next.

A chance to breathe and figure things out.

They had assured her there would be plenty of free time as the boat wasn't being chartered this season. It was being used exclusively by the owner instead, who cruised when the whim took him and didn't entertain too much or travel with a gang of freeloaders. But did insist on having a live-in crew at the ready at all times.

Which meant Tiffany might have time to pursue other things. Like that book that had been brewing in her head ever since she'd set foot on her first cruise ship and her romance with the ocean had begun. She'd been ignoring the urge for years but ever since Kelsey and Ari got hitched, it had thrust itself to the fore of her mind again.

They'd invited her to come and say with them in their apartment in Athens or the one in London, for as long as she needed. But Tiffany had financial responsibilities she couldn't let slide and the newlyweds already had Kelsey's mother living with them. They didn't need a fourth wheel.

She took a deep steadying breath, dragging warm Aegean air into her lungs before rolling her suitcase the short distance to the cast rail. Behind her was the waterfront where colourful tavernas, restaurants and souvenir shops bordered the cobble-stone promenade that separated land from water. Where donkeys – the only form of transport on the island – patiently waited with their handlers to deliver tourists to the Church of the Assumption, or their hotels or one of the seaside villages further away.

In front of her was her invitation to the sea.

Stepping onto the sleek, sturdy bridge leading from mooring to deck, she dragged her case behind her as she navigated the narrow path then stepped onto the aft lower deck area. No one appeared to be around to greet her, so Tiffany took a moment to imagine what it must be like to own something like this. To live this kind of life. To take off when you felt like it and drop in wherever you wanted. To have that kind of freedom at your fingertips.

To know you could cast off and travel anywhere the whim took you.

Not that she'd ever wanted to be rich. Having money – on paper anyway – hadn't brought her mother much joy, or helped her little brother fit into a hypermasculine world that didn't make space for vegetarians, especially those who preferred creativity to cattle. And God knew she'd seen enough tragic stories in the eyes of many a high roller who had sat down at her blackjack table.

But to have the time and space money afforded a person? That would be nice.

'Oh, hey.'

Tiffany turned at the sound of a thick Scottish accent to find a big guy with a shock of red hair and woolly red beard shot with grey. 'Hi.' She walked forward, extending her hand. 'I'm Tiffany. The new second stew,' she said as they shook. 'People call me Tiff.'

'Ivan,' the guy said, introducing himself with a smile. He was in black shorts and a navy polo shirt with *Nerida* embroidered in white on the left upper chest. 'I'm the bosun. My wife, Kelly, is the first stew. Come on in and I'll take you down to meet everyone then you can meet the boss.'

He grabbed her bag before Tiffany could assure him she was fine carrying it herself. She was big-boned like her father and brothers and strong from years of hard work lugging hay bail and saddles and roping cattle. But he took off at a clip and she followed as he strode through the boat, naming rooms as he went, travelling through the kitchen to a set of stairs that led below deck to the staff quarters. Everyone, dressed in variations of the Nerida navy shirt, was sitting at the staff dining table, so she got to meet them en masse.

Remembering names was not one of Tiffany's fortes but, in her defence, large cruise ships usually employed about two thousand people. And sometimes, like on her last ship, the *Hellenic Spirit*, turnover could be significant. She was pretty sure she could handle the names of five people.

'This is Tiff,' Ivan announced to the people around the table cradling mugs topped with frothy milk and indulging in a mid-morning snack, which appeared to be baclava.

Her stomach growled. She'd been too excited and nervous to eat this morning before she caught the ferry from Athens to Hydra.

A deluge of introductions followed. There was Maria, the chef from Venezuela; Kelly, a Kiwi who was the first stew and essentially her direct boss as well as Ivan's wife; Simon from Nova Scotia, who was another member of the deck crew along with Anja, who was Danish.

Tiffany smiled at each of her new crewmates. The mix of accents was one of the things she'd known she was going to miss about being on a huge cruise ship, but it appeared she needn't have worried.

'I'll take you to meet the boss when you're ready,' Kelly said as she showed Tiffany to her cabin.

It was a bunkbed but the space wasn't too cramped, and she didn't have to share with anyone – bonus. Stowing her suitcase on the lower bed, Tiffany turned and said, 'No time like the present.'

Kelly took her on a more thorough tour as they made their way up to the bridge, through the guest suites and saloon, bars and lounges, chatting all the way about their cruise to Mykonos tomorrow and what a cushy gig it was on the *Nerida*. When they got to the bridge, it was empty.

'Oh.' She frowned. 'He was here earlier. Hang on.' She unclipped the small handheld walkie talkie hanging from her hip. 'Boss, the new girl is on the bridge.'

Girl. Tiffany couldn't ever remember feeling like a girl. She'd been her father's little sidekick for years and then, at the age of twelve, she'd seen something she shouldn't have and she'd grown up overnight.

'Roger,' a distorted voice responded.

'He won't be long,' Kelly assured. 'In the meantime, this is the wheelhouse where—'

She was interrupted by Ivan's Scottish brogue over the radio. 'Kel, provisions have arrived.'

'Roger, I'll be down.' She slid the radio back in place. 'Do you mind if I...' She gestured her intent to leave.

'Of course.' Tiffany nodded. 'Go. Actually, why don't I come and give you a hand with the provisions? This could probably wait?'

One of the things Tiffany had liked about working on massive cruise liners was being one of many small cogs in a big wheel that all did their own thing to keep the ship rolling. Cogs didn't meet the owner of the wheel.

Not unless there'd been a serious screw up.

She understood this was a comparatively much smaller boat and that the owner was on board and that she'd probably run into him on a daily basis, but she wouldn't have thought people who owned multi-million-dollar superyachts generally hung out with their staff. It wasn't like they were going to be lounging in the jacuzzi together.

Their intro could surely wait.

Kelly quirked an eyebrow. 'Impressing the owner already, you'll go far.' But she was obviously teasing as she continued. 'At ease, sailor, there'll be plenty enough for you to do over the next two months. You can take this one off.'

Kelly departed out the same door they'd arrived, and Tiffany took a moment to glance around the space dominated by polished wood and dark leather. Her attention was drawn to a bank of screens that sat at right angles to what she presumed was the instrument panel, which was tucked just below the expansive windows that followed the curve of the bridge and afforded the captain a 180-degree view of wherever he was heading.

Hanging off the panel dead centre was an old-fashioned wheel. It wasn't pirate-ship huge but it fit the nautical ambience, its rounded wooden contours gleaming with polish.

As she lifted her eyes, Tiffany's gaze was drawn to the view through the spotlessly clean glass and the beckoning blue beyond, and her breath caught. It didn't matter how many times she saw the water in this part of the world, it always entranced her, even as she struggled to define the exact shade of blue.

The door on the other side of the wheelhouse opened abruptly, interrupting her musings. A strange prickle brushed her nape as Tiffany turned to find the owner striding in her direction. And that was when her stomach went into freefall.

Oh God. It was him. Theo Callisthenes – in the flesh. Wearing a hell of a lot more clothes than the last time she'd seen him.

Of all the gin joints in all the towns in all the world...

Tiffany saw the exact moment realisation dawned for him, his powerful stride breaking as he came to a complete stop. Two brows pulled down and froze into a dark slash above those piercingly blue eyes she hadn't been able to forget.

'*Tiffany?*'

Momentarily speechless, all she could do was stare. At the toss of his dark hair, the harsh cut of his cheekbones, the stubble darkening his square jawline, the jut of his chin. The fullness of a mouth that he'd known exactly how to wield for maximum effect. Not to mention those broad shoulders she'd clung to as he'd pounded into her, and those quads so perfectly delineated they could have been chiselled from marble.

Quads that had supported and cushioned her as he'd pinned her against the back of a hotel door and driven her to the most exquisite orgasm of her life.

If Tiffany had been superstitious she'd have wondered why the universe was conspiring to thrust them together *again,* but she was far too pragmatic for that. As ever, she preferred to get on with it.

'Theo.' She'd been going for nonchalant but missed the mark by a mile, her voice disappointingly high. 'Surprise.'

3

For a couple of charged beats, the heated slumberous glow in his eyes told Tiffany he was picturing the same images as she, from that night neither of them had slept until the sun had stretched golden fingers over the horizon. And for a crazy second, Tiffany thought he was going to break through his inertia, take a step forward, slide his hands on her hips and hitch her close.

But then his brows pulled down again. '*Oxi*.' He shook his head. 'No.' Then, '*Nomezo*.' Which she assumed meant double-no as he gave another shake of his head, tousling hair she could still feel silky smooth against her breasts and belly as he had kissed down her body. '*Apokliete*.'

Theo had whispered Greek to her in the throes of passion that had curled her toes. Low and gravelly, straight into her ear. Tiffany hadn't known what he was saying – she hadn't needed to; his tone had made it obvious they were hot and dirty, dredged from the deep cauldron of lust in which they'd been immersed.

She didn't need a translation for these words either. He didn't want her on the boat.

Tiffany couldn't decide if she was insulted or angry. But she was definitely blindsided. This was not the way she'd thought today would go down. Still, if he thought she was going to be a pushover, then he didn't know her at all.

It had been a month since a regular pay cheque and she needed the job. Sure, she could probably get another soon-ish but it was peak cruising-the-Isles-in-a-superyacht season and crews had already been set, which made it more difficult.

Money might grow on trees in his world, but it didn't in hers.

Also, she'd never been dismissed from a job before she'd even started, and that rankled. Coming from him it felt like a very specific rejection that had nothing to do with her abilities or her work ethic, and that really stuck in her craw. Tiffany drew herself up to her full five feet nine inches and injected steel into her spine.

'Yes.' No way was she going to be pushed out of a job because the guy in charge couldn't compartmentalise his life.

She crossed her arms to emphasise she meant business, but that just drew his gaze to her chest where the movement had plumped up a cleavage already generously displayed in her V-necked T-shirt. Her nipples ached beneath his lingering assessment as if remembering how perfectly he'd worshipped them.

Stupid nipples.

But then his mouth flattened into a grim line, and he finally found his feet. Giving her a wide berth, he crossed to the panel of instruments and Tiffany turned to see him consulting the screens and fiddling with a mouse.

'I'll call the agency and get you placed somewhere else and cover your expenses to get there,' he tossed over his shoulder.

Tiffany stared at his broad shoulders. So, she was... dismissed? Without even the courtesy of looking her in the eye? Yeah. Nah. As they said back home.

'No.'

His shoulders straightened, his head came up and Tiffany's pulse spiked as he slowly turned. His face was a formidable mask of prime alpha male, his eyes blazing blue heat, his clenched jaw brick hard. Not the face of the man who had smiled and flirted and charmed. This was the face of a man who was clearly not used to hearing no parroted back at him.

She supposed she was meant to feel intimidated. But Tiffany had grown up around men just like Theo. Okay, sure, they didn't wear suits or run companies, but they could out-alpha most men. They could rope a cow, ride a pissed-off bucking bull, fell a tree, string a fence, find water in a desert, make a roaring fire and build a shelter. All in one day. Men who'd be handy to have around in the apocalypse and didn't suffer fools gladly.

So, no, that look of steely determination didn't intimidate her. In fact, quite the opposite. It was strangely thrilling as their gazes clashed and sparks arced between them. How would *this* version of Theo Callisthenes bed her? She'd sampled the prowess of the charming playboy and been thoroughly sated, but she suspected the experience with the tight-lipped tycoon would be one hundredfold more intense.

Not that she had any intention of being bedded by the billionaire again. She was perfectly fine with their one-night thing staying a one-night thing, especially given her best friend had married his brother.

Of course, she'd known at the time because of Ari and Kelsey that her and Theo's path might occasionally cross in the future, but Tiffany had figured she could probably avoid most of those situations ahead of time. Would she have had sex with Theo had she known he was going to be her boss one day?

No.

Although technically, she supposed, he had been her boss

already. But she couldn't undo that now and she'd never been one to cry over spilt milk.

It was Theo's turn to cross his arms, but Tiffany refused to be cowed by his grim-faced resolve, meeting his gaze unflinchingly. 'So... do you want to tell Ari that you fired his wife's best friend on her first day or shall I?'

She hadn't planned on exploiting that connection but it clearly worked, the dark swathe of stubble across his jaw not hiding the shift of muscles as he clenched his teeth then muttered something in Greek Tiffany was pretty sure was not suitable for work.

'Did you know?'

Tiffany frowned. 'Did I know what?'

'That this is my boat.'

What the? Did he think she was... stalking him? Man, his ego was bigger than this whole damn superyacht. 'You think I *orchestrated* this?'

'Did you?'

'Because I, what...? Needed to get some more giant Greek dick in me?'

Behind a blackjack table, Tiffany took great pains to exude a quiet, dignified persona. She always wore her hair pulled back into a sleek bun, her uniform fitting her curves like a glove, oozing sexy competency. But away from the tables she was just a sheila from a cattle station who'd grown up around language that had never been suitable for little ears.

And she didn't have a problem pulling it out for maximum effect or shock value.

Unfortunately, Theo didn't seem shocked. He just smiled sardonically. 'You wouldn't be the first woman.'

Noting that he hadn't disagreed with her summation of what he was packing behind the zipper of his snug-fitting navy shorts,

Tiffany quirked an eyebrow. 'Am I supposed to feel sorry for you? Poor little rich boy with women fawning all over you?'

Well before her best friend had an illicit cruise ship romance with Ari Callisthenes, Tiffany had known all about Theo and his playboy reputation. As a long-time consumer of trashy European tabloid magazines, she'd glommed up images over the years of the dashing Greek billionaire and a string of different women.

He'd certainly never looked like he'd needed anyone's pity.

She had, though, felt a certain amount of affront on his behalf at those pictures that had appeared on the internet a couple of months back. A naked Theo with two equally naked women, taken through a half open doorway. Maybe because she knew him now, the invasion of his privacy had felt more personal.

What if that had been her in those pictures with Theo?

The thought of that twisted through her gut along with something else. A pang of something darker. Envy? Jealousy? Something she definitely had no right feeling. And couldn't afford to entertain.

'Did. You. Know?' he repeated, his smile thinner this time.

'Two things,' she said, returning his tight smile with one of her own. 'This might come as a shock to you but all I was interested in when the agency contacted me was the job description and location. The identity of the owner didn't cross my mind.'

Tiffany wished she could tell him point blank he hadn't crossed her mind for a single solitary second, but she wasn't that good a liar.

'Secondly, you might like to think I've spent the intervening months since our... very pleasant liaison' – it was satisfying to see her deliberate insult cause a flare of irritation in his eyes – 'penning deep and meaningful love letters and obsessively googling you, but... I haven't. Consequently, I didn't know you owned a boat.'

Two dark brows raised in blatant disbelief. 'I run a shipping company, I own dozens of boats.'

Tiffany shot him a derisive look. 'I think you know what I meant.'

'So that's a no, then?' he asked, returning to his original question.

'It's a no. Although I suppose the bigger question is, why didn't *you* know I was coming?'

He lifted one shoulder in a shrug. 'Kelly's responsible for the hiring and firing of the steward crew. I don't micromanage.'

Well, that was a lie. He'd micromanaged his ass off that night. His hands and mouth – lips, teeth, tongue – everywhere all at once, making sure no part of her was left wanting.

Regarding each other for long moments, neither of them said anything. His unwavering gaze held hers as surely as the frisson crackling the air pinned her to the spot.

'Did Ari send you?' he asked into the stony silence.

Tiffany was back to frowning. What the hell? And then realisation dawned. 'You're worried about your no-sex dare with Ari?'

Theo blinked. 'You know about that?'

'Of course. Ari told Kelsey. And because we're best friends' – also because Kelsey had a ridiculous fantasy about the four of them being all married up and having babies together ever since Tiffany had stupidly let slip they'd bonked at her wedding – 'she told me. That's what we do.'

Although, there were some things Tiffany hadn't shared about her life. Sure, she'd told her bestie about the night she'd spent with Theo – in very sketchy detail – and there was no way she was keeping *this* development to herself, but some stuff was too hard to tell.

'Kelsey tells me they're impressed by how invisible you've been since the dare.'

Knowing what she knew about Theo, and not just his well-documented tabloid sexploits over the years but first-hand knowledge of his appetites, she was also impressed.

He had been hiding away on a boat, though, so how hard had it really been?

'I guess it's an easy dare to take up,' she goaded. 'I mean, how exactly is it being policed? How is Ari to know if you break it?'

'It's an honour thing,' he ground out, his blue eyes unwavering on hers.

'So if you break it, you, what? Confess?'

His brows pulled down. 'I won't break it. But... yes. I gave my word. We shook hands. That's how honour works.'

There was derision in his voice, like he was pissed at having to explain integrity, and now it was Tiffany's turn to be impressed. Her gaze sought out any disingenuity in his implacable expression but there was none to be found.

Tiffany had known honourable men in her life. Some of the old stock men she'd worked with were ethical to their core. But she'd also known men who pretended to be honourable who acted differently when no one was watching. Her father being the prime example.

So, she knew the difference. And Theo, she believed.

Still, it had been a while for him. He must be feeling it? Emboldened and a little bit turned on by how tightly strung he must be right now, Tiffany ambled closer, trying not to think about how quickly she could get him off or wonder how much resistance he'd put up if she dropped to her knees and reached for his zipper.

Because he wanted her. She could see that. And she wanted him. With the same kind of desperation and inevitability she'd felt the first time they'd laid eyes on each other.

Would he beg her to put her mouth around him? Would he wrap her hair around his fist and guide her? Would he groan her name as he came down her throat the way he'd done in that hotel room?

Theo didn't back up but as she neared, she could see his jaw working. 'What exactly does this no-sex dare involve?'

Sex was a fairly broad activity, after all. Did it disallow fellatio? Or self-love? Drawing to a halt, a foot between them, she tipped her head back slightly to look him in the eye. 'Are there some guidelines?'

'No kissing. No nudity. No penetration.'

'No kissing?' Tiffany's gaze drifted to his full mouth momentarily before drifting back to meet his gaze. 'But that can be so harmless.'

'Not with me, it's not.'

It was a breathtakingly arrogant statement that she could back 100 per cent. The way he'd looked at her with such singularity and flirted with her so outrageously at the wedding had been exceptionally hot, but the second his mouth had taken hers against the back door of that hotel room, she was a goner.

Just the thought of it now made her hotter than she should be if she wanted to keep control of this conversation. Time to get back on track. 'So... it's been a couple of months, right? Is that why you want me off the boat? Afraid you'll crack, Theo?'

The knowledge was as dizzying as his cologne – aniseed and sea spray – the pulse in her neck fluttering wildly at the prospect that this rich, capable, commanding guy, who could probably have any woman in the world he set his sights on, saw her as a threat.

Meeting her eye, he smiled. Not with humour but with derision, his gaze cool now, the smoulder that had flared like a pilot light as she'd walked towards him firmly doused. 'I have full confidence in my self-control, Tiffany.'

She liked the way he said her name. Just a hint of an accent in his otherwise polished English. She'd invited him to shorten it but instead he stretched the double f like he was savouring it, rolling it around his mouth and enjoying the taste.

'Good then. Me being here shouldn't be an issue.'

'No issue,' he muttered as he fingered a tress of her loose chestnut hair.

Tiffany went deathly still as Theo's gaze homed in on it and he twined the lock around his finger. It might as well have been a loop of her intestine the way her gut clenched at the intimacy. 'How's *your* self-control?' he asked, glancing from his finger to her face, his voice so rough it was like the scrape of sandpaper along her bare arms.

'Rest assured, Theo, I'm not here to tempt you.'

Which was not what he'd asked, but Tiffany wasn't sure she could answer honestly without passing over a lot of power. And Theo Callisthenes was already powerful enough.

'I'm here to do a job. That's it. You need a croupier, and I'm very good at what I do.'

As he tugged his finger free, Tiffany's hair unspooled into a perfect curl. 'Isn't this boat a little small for you?'

Tiffany almost rolled her eyes. Why were men always so obsessed with size? She shrugged instead with as much nonchalance as was possible given their closeness and the way his cologne reminded her of how it had clung to her skin as she'd crept out of his hotel bed.

'I'm after something a little different,' she said.

'I thought you loved working on the big ships.'

She had. And had told him so at the wedding. And then

suddenly, she hadn't. 'I've been doing it a long time and I just feel...' She shook her head, her hair ruffling around her face. 'Restless, I suppose.'

'Yeah.' His blue eyes met her hazel. 'I know the feeling.' Another long pause followed, their gazes fully locked. 'Dare aside, Tiffany, I don't screw the crew.'

Was it wrong to be a little turned on by that phrase? Did that make her a terrible person? 'Excellent.' She nodded. 'Because I don't screw the boss.'

Not twice anyway.

'Okay then.' He held out his hand. 'Welcome aboard the *Nerida*.'

Tiffany shook perfunctorily, the zap of warmth up her arm warning her it might not all be calm sailing ahead...

4

Theo was still kicking his ass the next morning as he strode out onto the main deck aft where the crew were seated enjoying their breakfast. They had their own dining area below deck but Theo was more than happy for his live-in staff to have full run of the boat when no guests were on board, which meant he usually ate with them too.

Not yesterday though. He'd eaten his lunch in the wheelhouse and gone into Hydra to dine at a taverna for his evening meal, trying to forget the fact that he'd been goaded into letting the goddamn devil herself stay on board.

He'd called Ari as soon as he was clear of the *Nerida*. His brother was apparently surprised by the news too but also utterly delighted, laughing his ass off.

Malakas.

'This is perfect,' Ari had said between peals of laughter. 'You've had your tongue hanging out for her the moment you laid eyes on her in that blue bridesmaid's dress. And then you slept with her even though I warned you not to. You know what this is?' His brother had laughed again. 'This is karma. Because there's no way you'll be able to resist Tiff walking around the boat, especially after two months of celibacy, and then you lose.'

And that, along with Tiffany questioning his self-control, had made him even more determined to stay the course. Even if his balls were bluer than the fucking Aegean right now.

It seemed Ari and Tiffany wouldn't be happy until he'd blown a nut, but he couldn't hide away forever and he needed to go over the plans for the next few days with the crew. Also, Maria's lobster benedict was one of the best things he'd ever put in his mouth.

One of the other things was sitting at the table, all sparkly fresh, her hair pulled back into a low ponytail cinched at the nape, her navy Nerida T-shirt pulled taut across her generous chest.

Perfect. Just fucking perfect.

At least she was in the same uniform as everyone else, which was a very visual reminder that Tiffany was *staff*. Crew. And he was on a goddamn fucking sexual hiatus thanks to his annoyingly arrogant brother.

He pulled out a chair next to Simon as the crew greeted him, including Tiffany, who echoed their 'Morning, boss' demure AF, and Theo's stomach lurched at the word *boss*.

In line with everybody else, she'd started calling him that yesterday – when she called him anything at all – and he wondered if she knew how crazily his body reacted to the term. It felt ridiculous calling him that given their deep carnal knowledge of each other, and he wanted to tell her to stop. But another much darker part wanted to hear her say it when she was naked on her knees in front of him.

Yes, he was officially in hell.

Distracting himself with breakfast, Theo served himself two helpings of lobster benedict from the warming plate in the centre of the table and a mountain of perfectly cooked mush-rooms, attacking the food with gusto. After his call with Ari last night, he hadn't had much of an appetite and was, consequently, starving.

'Tiff tells us you two know each other,' Kelly said conversationally.

Theo glanced swiftly at Tiffany. He hadn't expected her to be candid about their prior relationship. In fact, he'd thought she'd probably not say anything, given the dynamics of a boat crew all living in such close quarters could sometimes get tricky.

But this way was better. He didn't like lying to anyone, even by omission. And he didn't want his crew to somehow find out another way. It would make it seem like he and Tiffany had colluded to keep it under wraps, which might lead them to wonder why.

'Yes. My brother is married to Tiffany's best friend.'

'That's an amazing coincidence,' Maria said, looking between the two of them.

Tiffany raised her mug for a sip as she said, 'It's a small world.'

She was being very polite and circumspect. Her polished cruise boat persona, he supposed. Not the wickedly candid, exceptionally funny and surprisingly potty-mouthed woman he'd first met at the wedding. Something she hadn't apologised for at the time. In fact, it had been almost like she was daring him to take exception to her rougher edges.

But if this last two months had proved anything, it was that Theo Callisthenes was always up for a dare.

Frankly, her take-me-or-leave-me act had been a novelty. And a woman not bending over backwards, not hanging on his every word or laughing at all his jokes and actually having an opinion, had been the clincher. Theo hadn't even been aware he was after a novelty. Until he woke to find the other side of the bed empty.

But there was definitely something about a woman who could say *giant Greek dick in me* – yeah, that had played on loop in his head ever since – without batting an eyelid.

And she was on his goddamn boat for the next two months.

'So, what's the plan, boss?' Ivan asked, turning his attention to Theo, who could have kissed the man's fuzzy Scottish face even if it did take him a second or two to decipher the accent. He was getting better at it but sometimes Theo only got every second word.

'We'll head straight to Mykonos after breakfast. That's about six hours. There are no berths available in the harbour so we'll anchor offshore, and Simon, you can take the tender tomorrow morning to pick up my guests.'

Simon nodded. 'Can do, boss.' His Canadian accent was a stark contrast to Ivan's and much easier to understand. Although the way he kept smiling at Tiffany was really fucking irritating.

'They're old friends from London who've been at some kind of international financial forum in Mykonos.'

Theo had attended university with them and he'd been working his ass off for two months to clear the decks for this week. Of course, he was still contactable if needed.

He was always contactable.

'And yes,' he said with a grin, 'by that I mean they're all pasty white English bankers.'

The crew, including Tiffany, laughed.

'So sunshine and island-hopping is definitely required. I'm keeping the schedule loose and making up my mind where we go at the start of each day depending on the weather. It'll be a start-stop journey, just dropping the anchor wherever looks good. They'll probably want to use the slide and jet skis I imagine during the days, probably tender over to whatever island is the nearest. Then at night—'

Theo finally glanced at Tiffany, who was regarding him over the rim of her mug. Just the sight of her across the table from him thrummed through his blood. It was hard to believe that after months of thinking and dreaming and fantasising about her, he could literally lean over and touch her.

He wouldn't have to shut his eyes any more – she was just there.

Hell, he could call her over the radio at his whim if he wanted. Not that he would because already that thought was conjuring all kinds of very unhelpful images about how she might obey – or disobey – captain's orders and what kind of punishment he might have to mete out for flagrant disregard of his instruction. Which was not only highly inappropriate, but the last thing he needed was a raging hard-on while talking schedules with his crew.

'That's where you come in. My friends, who seriously should know better given how much they know about money, like to gamble. So, I'm taking on a blackjack table and a roulette wheel as well and a tonne of chips in Mykonos. The saloon will become a makeshift casino for the week.'

One magnificently arched eyebrow lifted. 'Are they playing for sheep stations, as we'd say back home, or for bragging rights?'

'Bragging rights. Trust me, none of them need the money.'

'Thanks.' She nodded. 'Good to know.'

Theo swore he could see her calibrating her expectations as he watched. It didn't surprise him that she was taking everything in her stride. He'd pulled her personnel file at three o'clock this morning – no, he didn't care how dodgy it was – and found nothing but high praise for her work ethic and her ability to keep a cool head when things got tense around a table.

Not that she'd have to worry about that this next week.

Dragging his attention from her, Theo continued to outlay the plan. 'At the end of the week we'll be dropping them back at Piraeus and probably staying on in Athens for a bit while I attend to business. Then I think we'll head for Crete.' He looked around the table at each of his crew. 'That work for everyone?'

Technically, as boss, the opinion of his crew wasn't actually a factor in his decision-making. He was certainly nowhere near as egalitarian in the boardroom. But this wasn't a commercial charter situation which happened regularly throughout the tourist season when Theo wasn't on board and for which the crew were trained.

This was the owner entertaining friends, which meant it would be a more informal, relaxed trip for everybody. And, in his experience, a happy crew made for smooth sailing.

There was a round of nods as well as a wink from Simon in Tiffany's direction, which made her smile and made Theo's blood boil. Standing abruptly, he reached for a pastry off the central platter. It was light and flaky and he knew Maria would have cooked it fresh this morning, and it was a better choice than jabbing his elbow hard into Simon's ribs.

Addressing Ivan, he said, 'Departure in thirty?'

'Aye.'

And then, forcing himself not to look at Tiffany, Theo left them to it.

* * *

At ten thirty that night, Theo found himself on the main deck aft in nothing but a pair of shorts, a beer in hand, which he'd swiped from the bar fridge on the way through. It was a warm night and he was in holiday mode.

The crew had returned in the tender around eight after exploring Mykonos. He'd just stepped out of the shower but, even muffled, their happy, relaxed chatter told him they'd enjoyed their afternoon off. He hadn't gone out to greet them or check on them, staying in his suite, but he had heard the occasional noises as the deck crew had run all their usual night-time checks as well as Maria puttering around in the galley, which was not far from his suite.

Trying to distract himself from thinking about what Tiffany was doing, he'd caught up on some non-urgent emails and read through several files Ari had sent him for his signature until the noises stopped and silence had descended an hour or so later. The crew had obviously decided to turn in early given it would be their last chance for a week.

Theo knew he should probably sleep too – English bankers apparently turned into party animals on a Greek superyacht – but he wasn't sleepy.

In fact, he was back to feeling restless, again.

Preferring not to identify the reasons for this continued discombobulation, Theo had tried to channel it into work but had only been mildly successful when he'd given up an hour later. And so here he was, standing at the back rail instead, drinking beer and wondering yet again why he'd taken the bait and let Ari goad him into this ridiculous dare.

He sure as shit wouldn't be alone right now if he hadn't.

Although nor would he be on the *Nerida*, which he had enjoyed immensely these past two months. For the life of him he couldn't think why he hadn't opted for a floating office before. God knew there were all the bells and whistles he needed to run the company, and he was never far from shore in case he needed to get to the mainland for a meeting or an emergency.

Or a booty call.

Faint music from a nightclub on the promenade carried across on a light breeze, which ruffled his hair as Theo took in the lights of Mykonos. They shimmered across the water, popping from the shoreline and the hills behind as well as from the multitude of boats at anchor.

He knew the island well having spent many memorable times here as a kid. So fond were his memories of Mykonos that, when the Konstantinides controversy had hit the fan, he'd purchased one of the whitewashed villas that adorned the hillside behind the old town and holed away from a while. Ari had also lived in it for a time when he'd needed to shut the world out and wallow in his grief.

Unfortunately, he didn't get to visit it as often as he'd like but he loved that it had become the go-to place for family gatherings. Several times a year, the Callisthenes clan would crowd onto the large terrace overlooking the Aegean, marvelling at the view and taking advantage of the infinity-edged pool that cantilevered out from the hill.

There'd been many a good time over the years and Theo's long-term plan was to retire here. One day...

Apart from the distant music and the gentle lap of the sea against the hull, it was absolutely silent on the water, which Theo always found soothing. There was just something about being surrounded by an ocean. Its resilience was comforting. Civilisations had risen and fallen but it had always been here.

And then, at night, there were the stars.

Turning his back on the light pollution from Mykonos and the surrounding boats, he looked up to find them punctuating the inky night like strings of luminescent pearls nestled in black velvet. The sky had always been here too, and it wasn't going anywhere, either.

A clunk sounding overhead interrupted Theo's thoughts and he frowned. It had come from the sundeck. Something must have fallen because the crew had all retired to their cabins. Taking another swig of his beer, he pushed away from the railing and took the stairs to the sundeck two at a time.

It was dark up here too except for the low glow of strip lighting and the starlight. But Theo's eyes were adjusted to the night and he could easily make out the shape of a woman bending over, mopping something off the decking with a towel and cursing in a loud whisper.

'Fuckity, fuck, fuck.'

Tiffany. Of course. It had to be Tiffany.

Theo pulled up short as he stared at her ass which, given her current stance, was only just covered by a baggy T-shirt. He'd held that ass in his hands as he'd driven inside her, and God help him as he stood here staring like a fucking teenager, he remembered every soft, round contour. Hell, he still dreamed about how good it had felt in his palms.

Two things happened then. His cock, predictable as ever, did its thing and he was very pleased for the shadows of the night. But quite unpredictably, the nagging, twitchy feeling that had driven him outside evaporated.

Poof! Gone. Just like that.

5

'Need a hand with that?'

Tiffany jumped at the voice, her pulse spiking into the stratosphere. And not just because it was him but because she hadn't heard him approach or even known anyone else was around. She'd thought the peace and quiet up here was hers alone to enjoy.

'Bloody hell, Theo,' she hissed as she whipped around.

Finding him shirtless and barefoot did not help with the pulse situation. If anything, as her eyes were drawn to the coppery bronzed proportions of his chest – dark hair framing his pecs to perfection drawing the eye down to the puckered pillows of his abs – her heart climbed into her throat, making it exceptionally difficult to breathe. Which only kicked her heart rate up another notch or two.

He was rakishly sexy in the night, his wide stance – like he was the lord and master of all he surveyed – breathtakingly possessive. Even the ruffle of his hair in the breeze seemed orchestrated by nature itself to disarm. Give the man a flowy white shirt unbuttoned to the waist with frilly cuffs, a cutlass on his hip and skin-tight breeches tucked into bucket top boots and he'd be the full swashbuckling fantasy.

And Tiffany was today years old before she knew she had a thing for pirates.

'Sorry,' he murmured, although he didn't look sorry as his blue gaze drifted from the swell of her cleavage to the line where the hem of her shirt met her thighs before making its way back to her face. 'I didn't mean to scare you.'

Huffing out a breath, Tiffany glared at him. 'Well, you did.' She probably wouldn't have used that tone with any of her other bosses, but she hadn't blown any of her other bosses either so there was that.

Ignoring her glare, he took a drag of his beer and Tiffany hated how the movement of his throat as he swallowed drew her eye. 'Couldn't sleep?' he asked.

'No.' She'd been too restless. Nervous about making a good impression with their first guests tomorrow. That was what she'd told herself anyway, but looking at Theo, she realised that feeling had suddenly disappeared, and that made zero sense. Him going full Orlando Bloom on her should have cranked it up a hundredfold. 'You?'

He shook his head, his eyes holding hers. 'No.'

Dragging her gaze off him, she glanced at the towel she was carrying. She'd used it to mop up the red wine spill and absently hoped she'd be able to get the stain out. 'I hope it's okay?' Tiffany asked, ordering her arms and legs to work grateful when they complied moving her to the sun lounger she'd been sitting on. 'To be up here?' she clarified as she hung the towel over the back.

'Of course,' he said with a frown as he took in the open laptop lying on the lounge. 'You can have the run of the boat when there are no guests on board. Feel free to use the jacuzzi if you want.' He gestured to the rounded contours of the hot tub situated at the aft end of the deck to take full advantage of the water view.

'Thanks.' She may well take him up on that another night, but she certainly wasn't going to do it in front of her audience of one. Especially not when her body was still humming at the sight of him. The more clothes she had on in his presence – even if he did not – the better.

The baggy T-shirt she wore to bed was perfectly decent, coming to mid-thigh, but with the way his eyes had toured her body, Tiffany wished she was wearing a high-necked, floor-length Regency ball gown.

With a chastity belt.

'Please,' he said, gesturing to her laptop, 'continue. Don't let me disturb you.'

Hmph. *Too late for that, dude.* But Tiffany sat because her legs felt weird and reached for her laptop because it was something to do while she waited for him to depart, which he was apparently in no hurry to do.

'Can I get you' – he glanced at the empty wine glass sitting on the table beside the deck chair – 'some more wine?'

Tiffany frowned. Something was up with him tonight. It was her who should be doing the waiting, not him. 'No, it's fine.' She shook her head. 'It was mostly gone anyway.'

He nodded then prowled to the back rail and stared over it for a moment or two before turning around, planting his ass against the sturdy metal and taking another drag of his beer, regarding her over the rim as he swallowed. At least at this distance, she couldn't see the rhythmic movement of his whiskery throat.

But as the silence and his regard stretched, tension seeped into her muscles. 'Okay, what's wrong?' she demanded, snapping the lid of her laptop closed. Might as well tackle this head on. 'You're acting strange.'

Theo looked like he was going to refute it but stopped himself. 'I don't know.' He shrugged. 'I feel... restless. Like I can't settle to stuff, you know?'

Ooh yeah, Tiffany knew.

'And I don't know why because I'm usually so focused.' Theo shook his head as if he was both puzzled and disgusted with himself. 'Distract me,' he said, pushing out of his lean and ambling in her direction.

Like he was some bored Greek god ordering a servant to entertain him.

Annoyed at his imperious command, Tiffany had a good mind to jump to her feet and salute him with a snappy 'Aye aye, sir'. Distract him? FFS. Arrogant much? And besides, the last time they'd distracted each other, she'd ended up riding him like a cowgirl.

'Should I play you the lute, my liege?' she enquired with acid sweetness. 'Or perhaps juggle?' He laughed as he sat in the lounge beside her, but Tiffany was not amused. 'You're a grown-ass man, Theo,' she said derisively. 'Amuse yourself.'

She didn't give a rat's ass that he was the owner/captain or her boss. Just because she'd dropped her panties for him once didn't mean she was put on this earth to entertain him. The man was clearly surrounded by too many yes women. As any cursory glance at a tabloid rag would attest.

'Fine,' he muttered as he pulled the side lever, reclining the back of the chair a little. 'But fealty's not what it used to be.'

He drew up his knees and, pissed off at him or not, Tiffany could no more have stopped herself from checking out his thighs than she could have driven this damn boat. Taut bronzed skin overlayed the thick muscular core of his quads, a dark dusting of hair only adding to the sheer masculinity.

Okay, she should definitely leave now. Because he was far too close. Even with a foot between their lounges, she could easily reach over and slide her hand onto one of those thighs.

'So, what are you doing up on deck all alone after everyone's asleep, drinking wine with only your laptop for company? Are you watching *Sex and the City* reruns?'

Tiffany almost rolled her eyes. She hadn't seen a single episode ever of *SATC*. Not because she thought herself above it but because she'd missed it between her cowgirl years and world travel. 'No. But thanks for the stereotyping.'

He laughed into the warm air and it floated around her deliciously smooth feathering goosebumps up and down her arms. 'Okay, so you're what?' He rolled his head to the side. 'Scrolling social media? Online shopping? Watching make-up tutorials?'

Tiffany met his gaze with an arched eyebrow, annoyed anew. His eyes were sparkling and he was clearly enjoying a little light teasing. 'You know, Theo, you really need to get to know different women.'

He laughed, a hand falling to his stomach. 'Ouch,' he said around the lip of the bottle, his head returning to the midline as he tipped the beer up and drained the contents.

'Maybe,' she continued, even though she was pretty sure he'd been deliberately trying to goad her, 'I'm watching a tutorial on how to make a jet propulsion engine for my NASA project. Or maybe... I'm writing my thesis.'

He returned his attention to her, their gazes locking. 'Are you writing your thesis?'

No. But it sure as hell felt like it. 'Something like that,' she murmured, pulling her gaze from his to inspect the stars.

He laughed. 'That is surely a yes or no answer?'

Tiffany mentally squirmed at his reply and contemplated leaving again. He might be her boss and her one-time lover, but she didn't owe him any explanations. So why, conversely, did it feel good to be here with him, where the rustle and whispers of her restlessness hushed?

Where her doubts over whether she could actually do this thing fell silent.

'I'm... writing a book if you must know.'

A beat passed before he slowly turned on his side to face her properly. 'Really?'

Shrugging, Tiffany clarified. 'I'm trying, anyway.' She shook her head, not quite able to believe what she'd revealed to this man who was irritating and exasperating and who already knew too much about her. 'You're the first person I've ever told,' she admitted on a huff of released air.

Normally it was something she'd tell Mikey, her younger brother, who, as an artist, would have fully understood the self-doubt of a creative. But this was something she'd suppressed for so long it actually felt easier to tell a stranger.

Well... stranger *ish*, anyway.

She knew Mikey would be annoyed by her omitting to tell him first because they'd always been close, and he had a flair for the melodramatic, which meant he'd sulk first before coming around. But that wasn't what she needed the first time she spoke it out loud to someone else.

'Well, in that case,' Theo said, his voice rich with a slight husk that brought out more of his accent, 'I'm honoured.'

Okay, yeah. Tiffany swallowed. That was what she needed.

'What kind of book?' he asked. 'Fiction?'

Tiffany nodded, relieved and grateful that Theo hadn't raised an eyebrow over her announcement, just plunged straight into her fanciful author pipedream. He hadn't questioned if she knew what she was doing or even asked if she was worthy; he'd just accepted.

Now, all she needed was that faith in herself.

'It's a fantasy, I guess. Maybe romantasy? It's about mermaids and an ancient curse but it's set in contemporary times.'

Two eyebrows lifted. 'You know *Nerida* means mermaid in Greek, right?'

What? 'No.' Tiffany rolled on her side. 'Really?'

He grinned, his blue eyes flashing, and he looked just like the charming playboy from the wedding who'd had her under him within two hours of the I do's.

'Really.'

'Is there a story behind calling her that?'

'My grandfather – Yanni – used to tell me tales of the Nereids when I was a boy. They were stories his *pappou* had told him when he was a boy. Every year my family would travel to the village where he grew up on the island of Kalymnos and in the evenings, he'd take me down to the crumbling stone walls of the harbour where the old men were mending their nets and we'd sit with them as they told stories of seeing sirens on the rocks.'

He laughed and shook his head as if he couldn't quite believe he'd been sucked in by their tall tales, but Tiffany could tell the memories were happy ones.

'I'm sure they were embellishing just for me but I used to hang on every word. So' – he looked around the boat – 'when it came to naming her, it was a no-brainer for me.' Glancing at her, he asked, 'Why mermaids for you?'

'I don't know. Maybe because I grew up surrounded by land instead of water?' Balmain Downs was an eight-hour drive to the ocean. 'I remember, there was this old cowboy who worked for my dad for years. Bear, they called him, because he was built like a grizzly, or a brick shithouse as my brother Gordy would say.'

Theo laughed. 'I like it. I think I'm going to adopt that expression.'

'He had hands like meat cleavers and a big old raggedy beard. And he used to be in the merchant navy so he had this old faded tattoo of a mermaid on his arm he got at some port or other and sometimes, around the campfire at night, if he had just enough rum in him, he'd tell stories of hearing the siren songs when he was at sea.'

'And you'd hang on his word?'

Tiffany smiled at the surprising similarities in their very disparate backgrounds. 'Uh huh. And I'd go to sleep weaving tales about mermaids.'

'So, you've always been a writer?'

'Yeah... I guess? I think I've always had stories in my head. I was just too busy being my dad's little buckaroo to think they were anything other than my active imagination.'

Back in the days when her father had been made of gold and his praise had meant the world – it had been a shock to discover under all that pretty shine he had feet of clay.

'And then I stepped foot on my first cruise ship and looked out at all that water and it was like this portal opened in my brain and all these ideas came pouring out. Images that had been there from when I was a kid that had been kinda jumbled and indistinct were suddenly clear as a bell. I just knew it was a plot for a book.'

'How did that feel?'

She looked beyond his shoulder, remembering the emotions of that moment which had been revelatory. Pragmatic, practical Tiffany didn't indulge in something so amorphous – that was Mikey's territory. 'Scary,' she admitted. 'But also like I was... putting on an old pair of slippers.'

'And so you started writing?'

Tiffany laughed. 'God, no. Not really. I tinkered here and there. I kept notebooks. But... life was full and busy and there's absolutely no privacy and not a lot of space on a cruise ship to think, and it seemed... silly and superfluous, and honestly?' She brought her gaze back to him. 'Doomed for failure. But... it never went away either and then—'

She stopped abruptly, realising she'd been about to say *I met you. And then I met you. That's when the restlessness had started, this need for more.* But no freaking way was she saying that out loud. It was hard enough admitting it to herself.

Rolling onto her back, she shifted her eyes heavenwards once again. 'It suddenly became this imperative. Like my brain was telling me to start now or it'd never happen. So I didn't renew my contract with Ōceanós but I still needed to be able to support myself while I gave this writing thing a red-hot try so—'

'You couldn't go home?' he interrupted.

Tiffany almost laughed out loud. She'd burnt that bridge at eighteen. 'No.' Nor did she want to. The ocean had replaced the red dust in her veins, and she was fine with that.

The sharp probe of his gaze heated her profile as she hurried on. 'Then this job came up and it seemed a perfect balance between what I know how to do and more time and space to explore what I don't know how to do. Yet.'

'And still be surrounded by water.'

Tiffany nodded to the stars. 'Exactly.'

Theo didn't say anything, just rolled to his back as well, and they both stared at the constellations as Tiffany silently berated herself for talking too much. She'd said more words in the past ten minutes than she had in the entire night they'd spent together. So had he.

Not that it had been a night for talking. Their two hours of surface chit chat had always been a prelude to sex and they'd both known it.

'Did you ever think,' he asked, turning his head again to look in her direction, 'maybe it's more than coincidence you're here? Maybe it's fate?'

A shiver – the good kind – worked its way down Tiffany's spine at the statement.

'Maybe something out there, the muses perhaps' – he side-eyed the sky before returning his gaze to her – 'guided you here. To—'

The words cut off, the silence even louder for the abruptness, and for a crazy second, Tiffany thought he was he going to say *to me*.

'The boat. To the *Nerida*.'

For a woman who'd grown up in the hard world of beef cattle where things as fanciful as muses – as Mikey could attest – didn't exist, Tiffany liked the idea of that far, far too much...

6

Ignoring the question, Tiffany glanced his way. 'Tell me, Theo, are all Greek men this whimsical?'

Just as she hadn't answered his question, he didn't answer hers. He just grinned and rolled onto his back and stared at the sky again. So she changed the subject.

'What about you?' she asked. 'What did you want to be when you grew up?'

His mouth broke into a grin, which ruffled like the breeze through the muscle fibres low and deep in Tiffany's belly. 'Would it surprise you to know exactly what I'm doing?'

'Cruising the Greek islands in a giant phallic symbol of a boat?'

He laughed out loud and it was just what was needed to burst the strange sense of intimacy that had sprung between them as they'd shared stories from their childhood.

'You are hard on a man's ego, you know that, right?'

She rolled her eyes. 'Just as well you have the ego of ten men.'

He laughed again before he continued. 'Not the cruising, no.

Well, actually, yes, that too.' His hand moved to splay against his abdomen, which was exceptionally distracting. 'But I meant running the company.'

'Oh, come on.' It was Tiffany's turn to laugh. 'Surely little four-year-old Theodorus didn't want to run a multi-conglomerate.'

'Four-year-old Theo wanted to be whatever his beloved *pappou* was. I am the first grandson and he doted on me. Still does.' He broke into an unabashed grin. 'He says he doesn't have any favourites among his many grandchildren and great-grand-children, but that he did love me first. I was his shadow, his... how did you say it? Little buckaroo?'

Tiffany nodded, smiling a little at the very Australian word given a romantic twist in the hands of his slight accent. On paper, she and Theo could not be more different. Greek versus Australian. Billionaire versus working class. Owner of a mega-international company versus owner of things that could fit in two suitcases. Loving – from what she could gather – family versus complicated family. Yet they'd both had similar experiences in their childhoods, which somehow bridged those divides.

'He took me into work often, into the office and down to the port, introduced me to everyone and never considered me too young to learn anything. And when my father stood down due to ill health when I was twenty-three, I was ready.' He shrugged. 'I never thought about being anything else.'

As a child, Tiffany had thought she'd stay on Balmain Downs forever. She'd been born there and she'd figured she'd die there, too. Luckily, life on the land teaches a person to be adaptable. 'What would you do if you weren't CEO? If you didn't have Ōceanós. If you weren't a Callisthenes?'

Pursing his lips, he thought about it for long moments.

Possibly for the first time in his life if what he'd said about his CEO aspirations was true. 'I'd be a fisherman.'

Tiffany frowned. She'd been expecting a much grander answer. 'Do you mean own fishing trawlers instead of cruise ships?'

'No.' He shook his head. 'I mean just me, a small boat and the sea. Sitting with the old men in the evenings smack-talking about the tourists ruining the ambience and the football scores and the weather. A simple life.'

Okay, she definitely hadn't been expecting that. Or the image currently in her head of him similarly dressed to the way he was now – no shirt, no shoes – standing in the well of a bobbing boat, his hair blowing in the wind, his skin burnished to an even deeper shade of bronze from days in the sun, every muscle in his body rippling as he threw out a net.

Yeah, she could see it for sure. But... it was hard to believe.

'I don't think many of them are rich?'

'You think I can't not be rich?'

He sounded amused more than affronted as Tiffany made a show of looking around his superyacht. Nothing like the simple tin boats powered by outboard motors she'd seen puttering out to sea from the multitude of Mediterranean harbours she'd visited over the past seven years. 'I think you might find it a difficult adjustment.'

Theo wasn't like his grandfather. He'd been born into money.

'Maybe,' he laughingly conceded. 'But I think I could be happy. Sun on my face, fish in my belly. Walking to work, the sea surrounding me? There are worse things.'

'True.'

There were. And it sounded idyllic. She could certainly picture herself sitting with her back to the harbour wall, laptop balancing on her knees, sun sparkling on a crystal blue ocean, as she weaved her mermaid stories and waited for her fisherman to bring home his catch.

Which was why she definitely had to leave. *Now!*

Lurching forward, she grabbed her laptop and stood. 'I'm going to turn in.'

'I'm sorry, I interrupted your writing.'

'It's fine,' Tiffany assured, not quite meeting his eye as she busied herself, shoving the computer under her arm, grabbing the stained towel with one hand and the empty wine glass with the other. 'I'm just in the planning stages. It's all good.'

She threw the towel over her shoulder to quell the sudden urge to tug the perfectly decent hemline of her oversized T-shirt lower. 'Well...' Clearing her throat, she tipped her chin in the direction of the stairs. 'Goodnight.'

Theo's softly spoken *'Kalinyhta,* Tiffany' followed her all the way to her cabin.

* * *

'Theodorus, you good-looking bastard.'

Theo laughed as the first of his London friends stepped on board from the tender. 'Jealousy is a curse, Rufus,' he said as they embraced.

Hugo, Ben, Fabian and Irving all followed to much backslapping and smack talk. 'Aha,' Rufus said, his gaze falling on Kelly, who was also there to greet their guests with a tray of beers. 'This is Kelly,' Theo introduced.

'And what a treat you are, too,' Rufus said, in full flirt mode.

For a guy who looked like he'd fallen from the ugly tree and smashed into every branch on the way down, Rufus always scored well with women. That could of course be because he had a lot of money, oodles of charm and one of those evenly modulated British accents that women apparently went gaga for.

The castle in Yorkshire didn't hurt.

No one ever took a picture through his French doors though because the difference was, Rufus had made his fortune behind the scenes and was able to remain anonymous.

Rufus and Fabian were the only two unattached members of the party. Ben was married to Patrice. Hugo was married to David. And Irving had been with an American girl called Neve since last Christmas.

'Dial it back, man,' Theo chided good-naturedly. 'Unless you want her giant Scottish husband who is up top readying the boat for departure to make your ball sack into a sporran.'

Rufus winced slightly and the other guys laughed as they each took a beer. 'Could I take him?' he asked Kelly conspiratorially.

She laughed. 'Depends how fond you are of your ball sack, I guess.'

More male laughter as they all moved up to the main deck where Maria had laid out a fresh batch of baclava. 'Tuck in,' Kelly said. 'Tiff will be here soon to give you the tour.'

The guys needed no further instruction, wolfing it down in five minutes flat as Simon bought up their bags from the tender. But just the mention of her name pulled Theo's stomach muscles taut AF. Their paths hadn't crossed since last night given the staff were now in guest mode, which meant they'd eaten breakfast in the crew mess and they'd been busy making last-minute preparations while he'd been plotting a rough course for island-hopping all the way to Santorini on the nav system.

But that didn't mean he hadn't been thinking about her non-fucking-stop since their tête-à-tête on deck last night.

Theo had never been particularly interested in the backstories of the women he'd taken to bed. He took great pains to keep everything superficial, and yes, he knew that made him a *kavliaris*, but it wasn't like he'd ever pretended otherwise. Or that said women gave a crap about his backstory either.

When he was between the sheets, his sole focus was on sending his one-and-done away with a smile on her face.

And the same had been true for Tiffany. But then he'd woken to an empty bed, a head full of sexy memories and her scent all over his body, and he hadn't been able to stop thinking about her. Had her Cinderella act been a challenge to his masculinity? Maybe. Was he butthurt that she was the first woman ever who had done the walking? Possibly. But then she'd turned up on the *Nerida* and he'd known the issue was much more complex.

Which had only been hammered home on the deck last night. Because not only had he wanted to know everything about her, but he'd wanted her to know everything about him.

And that was a first.

Not to mention how he'd jerked off to visions of her as a cowgirl complete with hat and fringed vest swirling a lasso around her head. Was he proud of that? Not particularly. But this last twenty-four hours, this fucked-up, no-sex dare had felt like an especially heavy yoke around his neck. Which, surprisingly, it hadn't been. Out here on his boat, he actually hadn't missed the merry-go-round of women or the constant paparazzi attention.

And then Tiffany had stepped on board and he was suddenly aware of every celibate hour of the last two months.

As if he'd conjured her from the febrile roil of his thoughts, Tiffany appeared just as the last dregs of the first beers had been

chugged down, and Theo could suddenly feel the dull thud of
his pulse everywhere.

She was wearing the more formal white shirt with black
epilates embellished with gold embroidery as Kelly had been, in
line with protocol. Crew were required to wear different
uniforms for different tasks: whites for greeting new arrivals and
for sendoffs, and their everyday uniform – navy branded T-shirt,
black shorts – throughout except for night-time dining, when
the steward staff wore black, be it a dress or a shirt/skirt/trousers
combo.

This was the first time he'd seen her in her whites, and fuck
if he didn't want to take her somewhere private and pop every
single one of those brass buttons. And wrap her high ponytail
around his hand and tug. And no matter how much he told
himself this was the result of two months without the company
of a woman, he knew that was bullshit.

This was about her. It was Tiffany.

'Gentlemen.' She beamed at his friends, and Theo wanted to
tell her to stop. Which he imagined would go down like a lead
balloon. She was supposed to be friendly and charming. She
was doing her goddamn job! 'I'm Tiff. If you're done, I'll show
you to your suites. Please, follow me.'

Turning slightly, she gestured to the door, which set her
ponytail in motion, swinging back and forth like a fucking magi-
cian's watch, deepening the spell she seemed to have cast over
Theo's goddamn libido.

Rufus, as quick and pompously charming as ever, bowed
deeply. 'My lady, I'd follow you to the ends of the earth. Unless' –
he paused for dramatic effect – 'you also have a big Scottish guy
who might punch me in the face?'

A white-hot flare of possession drove a hot spike through
Theo's brain. *He* wanted to punch Rufus in the face. And Fabian.

They were both smiling at Tiffany like she was the best thing that had happened to them today, and he wanted to growl, *back off, she's mine.*

Watching Simon flirt with her yesterday had been irritating, but some of his closest friends? That was pure fucking torture.

'Me?' Tiffany laughed. 'I don't need a big guy, Scottish or otherwise. I grew up with four brothers and a bunch of tough old cowboys as uncles. I have a pretty mean right hook.'

'A woman who can take care of herself.' Rufus clutched his chest. 'Where have you been all my life?'

Red mist swirled in front of Theo's face, his stomach a tight knot. 'Jesus, Rufus,' he snarled. 'Save it for the tourists on the islands and lay off my staff.'

That ponytail swung again as a startled Tiffany stared at him. Then, one by one, his five friends glanced from him to her and back to him again, speculation rife in their eyes, and Theo gave himself a mental kick. He might as well have lifted his leg and pissed at her feet.

Rufus, not at all chastised, saluted, a smug grin on his face. 'Aye aye, Captain.' Then he turned to Tiffany and said, 'Lead on, sweet lady, and do tell us all about yourself.'

Theo ground his teeth. It was going to be a long fucking week.

* * *

Still brooding several hours later, anchored off Naxos, Theo took a guzzle of his beer as he stood at the rail on the main deck, his foot on the middle rung, and watched Rufus and Fabian chase each other on the jet skis. Irving and Ben were lazing on the floating pontoons off the back of the boat after spending the last couple of hours throwing themselves down the large inflatable slide that was anchored on the main deck and hung off the side of the boat.

He watched as Tiffany, barefoot, navigated the floating surface, which bobbed as she walked to bring them an ice bucket jammed with beers. It was a tricky balancing act but she was managing more than admirably, that damn ponytail swinging.

'Thanks, Tiff,' they said in unison as she put it between them.

'You are a goddess,' Ben added.

She laughed. 'I bet you say that to all the women bringing you beer on a superyacht.'

'Of course,' he deadpanned. 'My wife would kill me if I didn't.'

They all laughed then, Tiffany tossing her head, the ponytail a-swinging once more as she turned and made her way back to the boat. Theo's mouth tightened, stupidly jealous of his friends able to enjoy the September ambience of the Aegean while his stomach was tied in knots, his thoughts churning.

Hugo, who sat on the board of several renowned financial institutions and had made a fortune on the stock market, sidled up beside Theo and they both watched Tiffany cross the last few metres of pontoon. Glancing up, she noticed them, giving a sunny wave, which Hugo returned and Theo did not.

'Tiff seems nice,' he said conversationally.

Of the five guys who'd boarded this morning, Hugo had known Theo the longest, which he used for good and for ill. Like now. Theo shot him a doleful look. 'There's nothing going on if that's what you're thinking,' he said, his voice not inviting any further inquiry.

But what were friends for if not to stomp all over the keep out signs? 'Okay.' Hugo shrugged. 'Sure.'

Which was irritating AF. 'Her best friend is married to Ari.'

'Ah.' Hugo nodded sagely.

Theo's foot slid from the rung as he turned to face his friend, leaning his hip into the railing. 'What does *ah* mean?'

'Nothing.' Hugo shook his head as he took a chug of his water. 'Just interesting that she's working on your boat.'

'It was a coincidence.'

'Or, you know.' He shrugged. 'The universe working in mysterious ways.'

Theo would have rolled his eyes at that had he not said something similar last night. Turning back to the water, he bent at the waist and braced his elbows on the top rail. 'I don't screw the crew.'

'That's a very good policy.' Hugo clapped him on the shoulder then mimicked his stance, and for several moments they both tracked the jet ski antics before he spoke again. 'Haven't seen your face or your cock' – he grinned broadly, obviously still amused at that picture – 'in any tabloids lately.'

Theo tensed. Like he wasn't already wound as tight as a fucking top. 'I'm taking a break.'

Hugo burst into laughter then. *Malakas*. 'I can tell from your mood it's clearly working out well for you.'

Theo's lips pressed together. 'I need the goddamn paparazzi off my back.'

Shaking his head, Hugo said, 'You always were all or nothing.'

'What the hell is that supposed to mean?'

'Have you ever thought that if you stopped being the one-and-done guy and actually saw a woman more than once, they might lose interest?'

No. He'd never thought that, but maybe Hugo was on to something. Maybe that was the issue with Tiffany. Just because he'd never met a woman he wanted to see twice, didn't mean she didn't exist, right?

Maybe Tiffany was that mythical unicorn. Maybe she was the two-and-done.

And maybe, once he'd won this ridiculous no-sex dare, he could see if she was interested in one more roll between his sheets. Because maybe he just needed one more time with her and then he could be done. Maybe that could fix everything.

For the first time since Ari's wedding, Theo could see a way out of this funk.

'You know.' Hugo half turned, leaning into an elbow. 'Not all women are Angelika Konstantinides.'

It was delivered quietly and sincerely, the way only an old friend could, but it hit like a sledgehammer. Theo was trying to figure out how to respond when Irving called to them from the pontoon. 'What the fuck are you two doing up there?' he demanded. 'Stop gossiping and get your asses down here.'

Theo, grateful for the interruption to the amateur psycho-analysis, didn't need to be asked twice. He clapped Hugo on the shoulder. 'Let's go.'

7

Theo almost swallowed his tongue when he and the guys entered the saloon at nine that night. And it wasn't because of how the wood-panelled room had been transformed into a casino thanks to Kelly's superior event-styling skills but because of the woman waiting for them behind the roulette table.

'Good evening, gentlemen.'

Tiffany – her hair pulled back into a tight, sleek bun, her croupier uniform the whole *Casino Royale* wet dream – smiled demurely through lips that were a rich glossy red, like she'd just walked out of a Robert Palmer video clip. She looked prim and proper and untouchable. The perfect evening hostess. Like nothing could ruffle her.

Like a true professional.

Like she hadn't opened her legs for him within two hours of their acquaintance and demanded he fuck her.

And *Christe,* if that wasn't hot enough to boil his eyeballs in their sockets.

Rufus whistled appreciatively. '*Enchanté,*' he murmured. 'You're making me feel exceptionally underdressed, Tiff.'

Given the lingering warmth of the evening, all six men were still in their attire from dinner, which was variations of shorts and T-shirts.

'Ditto,' Fabian agreed.

Another demure smile. 'T-shirt or a tux doesn't make any difference to me, I'll happily take your money.'

Everyone but Theo laughed. 'Ah, fighting words, I like.' Rufus cocked an eyebrow at Theo. 'She is such a delight, isn't she?'

Theo gritted his teeth at the devilment in Rufus's eyes. The rate he was going he'd have ground them down to stumps by the time they returned to Athens. Ever since he'd snapped at Rufus this morning, the guys had smelled blood in the water, and in that unguarded moment, Theo had shown his hand. They were used to seeing him with women; they weren't used to seeing him act like a dog guarding a juicy bone with any of them.

He'd revealed to them what he hadn't been willing to admit to himself – he was seriously into Tiffany Wainwright. And they were going to be relentless.

Theo's gaze slid to Tiffany looking all cool and controlled and *you can't touch this* in her collared white and red pin-striped blouse, the long sleeves ending in broad cuffs at her wrists, the bodice tight. Her dove-grey, narrow-strapped vest skimmed around the outer curve of her breasts to button just under them, framing their fullness to perfection.

Finishing off the ensemble, a large bowtie the exact colour of the pin-stripes nestled against her throat at the juncture of her two collar points.

And Theo wanted nothing more than to reach across and tug it open.

He recognised it as the uniform worn by all female croupiers on any of the Ōceanós cruise ships. No wonder so many men lost money at their tables. Hell, had he known that Tiffany looked this damn good in it, he'd have found it impossible to resist staying a night or two on the *Hellenic Spirit* just to sit down at her table.

Despite his one-and-done rule.

'She's a real treat,' he murmured, his gaze meeting hers. A treat he wanted to steal away to his suite, tear away her wrapping and gnaw on at his leisure.

A barely discernible lift of her right eyebrow told Theo she knew exactly what he was thinking before her gaze slid to Rufus. 'Well, gentlemen, why don't you head over to the bar and grab a drink and I'll get you set up with some chips.'

'Mmm,' Fabian said, winking at Theo. 'Bossy, too.'

Theo narrowed his eyes at Fabian, who merely smiled. Bastards were going to have a lot of fun at his expense. After all, who knew better than good friends how to really push buttons?

Although not, as it turned out, as much as Tiffany in that damn tie.

'I think,' Irving announced, looking around, 'this is giving martini vibes.'

With a ceiling covered in red and black balloons, cocktail glasses full of red and black dice and thick gold rope looped to form an official-looking VIP section, the saloon had been transformed.

'Shaken not stirred,' Ben agreed heartily. 'Is that possible, Kelly?'

Behind the bar, Kelly smiled. 'Shaken, stirred or dirty as you please. Everything is possible.'

Theo meandered to the bar with his friends as Kelly served drinks and they boasted about their prowess at the table and the wins they'd had, but Theo was far too distracted to be paying much attention to the smack talk. Tiffany had stepped out from behind the table to reveal the skirt of her uniform, which should surely be illegal anywhere on sea or land.

It wasn't that it was short because, coming to just above her knee, it clearly wasn't. Or that she was poured into it although, God help him, she wore it like a second skin. It was the way she walked in it as she paced back and forth between tables, swinging her hips in that way men didn't.

Purely subconscious but utterly female.

And how it flared out from the cinch of her waist to encase an ass a man could hold on to and thighs he could happily drown in. Thighs that belonged in a Rubens painting.

Then there were her calves and the way her six-inch, black, fuck-me stilettos set them off, the muscles bunching and loosening with every footfall, the action almost as mesmerising as the swing, swing, swing of her hips.

'What do you reckon, Theo?'

Dragging his attention back to the bar, he faced five – six, if he counted Kelly, who also seemed to be picking up the vibe he apparently couldn't stop putting down – amused expressions waiting for his response. With no idea what they'd been talking about, he quickly scanned their faces and took a punt. 'I agree,' he said with a nod.

Everyone laughed as Hugo handed him his martini. 'Good guess.'

* * *

Three hours later, the evening was winding down with just Rufus and Theo holding chips as they played another round of poker. Aside from the undercurrent buzzing between her and Theo, Tiffany had enjoyed herself immensely. With only six people to worry about and keep track of at the table, it was the easiest croupier job she'd ever done, especially with the increasingly tipsy Englishmen placing wilder and wilder bets.

It had been like taking candy from a baby.

Theo's friends were funny and charming, and it was evident from their camaraderie and their stories how close they were. They teased each other mercilessly and it was interesting seeing Theo in a different light as he laughed at the shared anecdotes.

She'd already seen the playboy who had shamelessly flirted with her at the wedding making no secret of his attraction. She'd seen the boss. The singular alpha one who had ordered her off the boat, the egalitarian one who had eaten with the crew and the off-the-clock one who had told her about his *pappou*. And now she was seeing him as the uni friend, and the clear affection these men held for him – not because of his money or his rep or his bloody great superyacht, but because of their shared history – told her more about him than any night spent between his sheets.

About the kind of person he was. And hell, if that didn't sit far too pretty in her brain.

'Waiting on you, sir,' Tiffany prompted Rufus, even though she knew he had a hand full of rubbish and Theo was sitting on three kings.

Because of course he was.

But even as she concentrated on the baby-faced banker, she was aware of Theo's gaze fanning across her like a lighthouse beacon. Aware of how it lingered on her throat and filled her with the irrational urge to strip off her tie so she could breathe properly. It seemed to cinch a little tighter with every passing minute. How was it possible to be surrounded by five other people – and yet feel like it was just her and him in the room?

It was insane, this chemistry between them. This physical

pull she felt in his presence. If she'd known this was going to be the result of their one-night stand, she'd have passed on the job.

Probably.

'Tiff, have I told you about that time Theo—'

'Rufus.' Theo glared at him. 'Quit stalling. Piss or get off the pot.'

Clearly unconcerned by Theo's objections, Rufus continued. '—got an old-lady ass-kicking on the streets of Holborn?'

Tiffany laughed before she could stop herself, grateful for the reprieve from Theo's heated intensity. Now, *that* she would like to have seen. Ignoring Theo and the waves of disapproval rolling off his body, she said, 'You did not.'

'But you want me to tell you, right?'

Tiffany shot a quick look at Theo, all stern and forbidding, and hell if her stomach didn't lurch. But she'd be damned if she let him see how much his presence tonight was disturbing her, and anything that could take Theo Callisthenes down a peg or two was welcome. Smiling with faux sweetness at her boss, she returned her attention to Rufus.

'You betcha,' she confirmed.

The guys cheered and drummed their hands on the table as Theo grimaced. Completely ignoring his friend's displeasure, Rufus launched into the story. 'I think we were about nineteen.'

Nineteen. It was hard to imagine Theo as a teenager when, in her mind, he'd always be the suave, sophisticated man that exuded the kind of ease and confidence that only came with age. That came with having lived and experienced.

'He and I had just come out of a pub we used to frequent where'd we'd had a cheeky pint—'

'I had a pint,' Theo interjected. 'You had several.'

Ignoring Theo, Rufus continued. 'And there was this older lady—'

'Ethel,' Hugo interrupted.

Tiffany glanced at the men. Clearly this was a story that had been told and retold. Possibly even gone down in legend between the six of them.

'Ethel,' Rufus said with a nod, his chips clinking as he fiddled with them. 'She was probably twenty-feet in front of us in this big old coat, a little hat with a feather perched on her head and this old-fashioned handbag – kinda like the Queen used to carry – swinging from her fingertips.'

'And a frilly pink umbrella hooked over the other arm,' Irving supplied with a grin. Clearly that was an important detail.

'Right,' Rufus confirmed. 'It had been raining on and off all day and it was freezing. Which also meant there weren't many people about. Then this guy comes from a side alley, walking towards her and snatches her handbag. It all happened very quickly. She yelps and before we know it, he's sprinting past us.'

'But Theo, with his cat-like reflexes, sticks out his foot at the last moment,' Fabian whispered dramatically.

Tiffany remembered how much Theo had reminded her of a jungle cat at the wedding. The way he'd prowled towards her with utter intent. *But Jesus, do not think about that now.* Giving herself a mental shake, she smiled at Rufus. 'You don't have cat-like reflexes?'

'Well... I was a little worse for wear.'

Theo snorted. 'You could barely walk in a straight line.'

'Anyway,' Rufus continued, unconcerned by all the interruptions. 'The thief falls on the ground and Theo jumps on him, trying to retrieve the handbag, but he's not giving it up without a fight. Then Ethel, who is wearing these Coke-bottle glasses, stalks over and all she can see is Theo's hand on her bag so she starts bashing him over the head with the umbrella, demanding he give it back. So now poor Theo's trying to grab the bag and ward off the umbrella attack.'

The guys cracked up and Tiffany joined them, the mental picture tickling her sense of humour. 'And what were you doing throughout all this?' she asked Rufus when everyone's laughter had settled.

Another snort from Theo, who was now crossing his arms. 'Laughing his ass off while I was being handed mine.'

Unabashed by his lack of action, Rufus grinned. 'I swear to you, Tiff. I was laughing so hard I almost fell over.'

Theo shook his head. 'Why are we friends again?'

'Because.' Rufus wriggled his eyebrow. 'I'm endearingly charming.'

Theo didn't deign to answer as Tiffany waited for the conclusion. 'Well?' she demanded from the grinning men. 'What happened next?'

'With all the commotion,' Rufus continued, 'the thief decides to cut his losses and escape, leaving Theo with the bag.'

'And once I had two hands,' Theo said, supplying the rest, 'I was able to disarm Ethel and give her bag back.'

Tiffany glanced in Theo's direction. The funny anecdote had given her a break from the weight of his gaze, and she felt like she could breathe again. 'Were you injured?'

'Only his pride.' Ben sniggered, which caused another round of laughter.

'Oh, but you haven't even heard the best bit.' Rufus grinned anew. 'Ethel insisted on rewarding him and wrote him a cheque for five pounds. Him.' He pointed at Theo. 'She refused to take no for an answer.'

Tiffany pressed her lips together at the thought of Theo, the heir to a Greek shipping line who'd just wrestled a frilly pink umbrella off an elderly woman, taking a paltry cheque for his troubles. 'Did you spend it wisely?'

Theo rolled his eyes. 'I donated it to a charity. Now' – clearly done with the topic, he picked up his cards again – 'if you're ready, could we get back to finishing this game?' He turned those blue eyes on Rufus. 'I believe it's your call.'

Rufus pushed all his chips into the centre. 'I'll see you and I'll raise you all of this.'

Theo flipped his cards over to reveal his kings. Rufus grinned as he turned his over to reveal a whole lot of nothing. 'You got me.'

Everyone groaned. 'You suck at poker,' Fabian muttered.

'Yeah, but I excel at bluffing. Now.' He picked up his glass of whisky and addressed his fellow guests. 'I think it's time we turned in for the night so poor Tiff can get to bed.' Eyeballing each man individually – except Theo – he threw his drink down.

One by one, they followed suit, the heavy tumblers making soft thuds as they were placed on the padded felt edge of the card table. One by one they bade Tiffany goodnight. One by one they shuffled off.

Until there was just her and Theo.

8

Tiffany watched as Theo strolled to the bar, tumbler in hand, and helped himself to the decanter of whiskey that Kelly had left out before she'd knocked off for the night. She'd already cleared and washed up the used glasses, leaving only the tumblers for Tiffany to take care of before she finished her shift.

'My hero,' she murmured, forcing herself to be nonchalant as Theo poured amber fluid into the heavy crystal. The saloon was not a small room but it suddenly felt suffocating – certainly not big enough for the two of them as the sound of liquid splashing into his glass filled the silence.

He chuckled. 'I think it would be slightly more heroic had I not been bashed with an umbrella by an old lady.'

Tiffany smiled as she picked up the tumblers that were sitting around the edge of the table. 'But you got her bag back.'

Sure, the story had been amusing but also intriguing in that it had given her further insight into Theo. Maybe it had been reflexes or the foolhardiness of youth, but he'd done something, he'd acted, where a lot of people might not have – without any thought to the consequences.

That wasn't nothing.

'True,' he conceded as he gestured to the decanter, his eyebrows raising in question. 'You want one?'

Tiffany had learned in her teens if a woman wanted to hold her own with the guys on an outback property, she needed to know how to shoot whisky. And rum. After a half dozen tinnies. And that had held her in good stead for her partying around Europe stage and for the many, many parties held in crew bars on cruise ships.

It had also helped her forget what was happening at home. But this wasn't that.

This was just a standard debrief session about how the night had gone. Could they improve on the experience for the guests or change anything up? Did Theo want to try anything different tomorrow night? Etcetera, etcetera.

'No. Thank you.'

'It's okay,' he murmured, a slight smile playing on that wicked mouth, his blue eyes dancing with humour below the fringe of his black brows. 'You're off the clock now.'

Off the clock or not, it was best not to lose any of her inhibitions around this man.

'Thanks, but no.' Glasses in hand, she crossed the saloon to the bar, giving Theo a wide berth as she slipped behind and placed her load beside the sink.

Putting in the plug, she flicked on the hot water, excruciatingly conscious of his gaze boring a hole in her back. Heat flared between her shoulder blades, along the ridges of her hip bones and around the base of her spine, each entry point burning all the way through to her front, licking at her nipples and undulating fiery fingers along muscles fibres that stirred a dull throb between her legs.

Her bowtie cinched a little tighter.

'You can do that in the morning if you like? You haven't even had a restroom break since we started and you are off the clock.'

'It's fine.' Tiffany shook her head. 'I don't mind.' It gave her something to think about other than the six feet two inches of pure man mere metres away.

Once the sink was half full, she turned off the tap and dropped the glasses in before heading back to the tables. 'Was tonight what you hoped?'

She clocked him turning in her peripheral vision, lounging back against the bar, his arms spread wide, his bent elbows resting along the top, the glass dangling from his fingers.

Even in shorts and a T-shirt it was commanding, and she was hyperaware of his attention as he tracked her progress across the room, the air between them sizzling.

'I think the guys had a blast.'

'And you?' she asked, deliberately not looking at him in case he saw something in her gaze she didn't mean to give away. Like how much she wanted him to have had a blast. This man who wrestled bag snatchers to the ground for little old ladies.

Reaching under the table, she removed the chip containers from the ledge, and started to sort the messy piles into towers according to their monetary value.

'Are you kidding? I could watch you rob my friends blind every night.' He chuckled and it was all low and sexy and felt conspiratorial. Intimate.

Like they were sharing a secret.

Tiffany glanced up from her sorting and met his gaze, which lingered on her mouth. 'You want me to take it a little easier on them?'

Tiffany played the way she would have played had she been on the *Hellenic Princess* – conceding some hands, getting them comfortable, getting them hooked then reeling them in.

Because the house always won.

But this wasn't a massive cruise ship with high rollers and even higher stakes. It was a superyacht with five fun, drunk Englishmen.

Pushing off the bar, he ambled towards her and Tiffany's breath drew shorter with every footfall. Halting when he reached the opposite side of the table, Theo placed his glass on the table edge. 'On the contrary,' he murmured as he raked over a pile of chips. 'It's probably the only payback I'm going to get for their endless embellished stories over the next six nights, so go for it.'

Despite the tension from his proximity tightening every muscle in Tiffany's body, she laughed. 'In that case, sir, I will be merciless.'

Tiffany didn't mean for it to be flirty – not consciously, anyway – but the flicker of blue flame in Theo's eyes told her it had been. His gaze drifted to the knot of her tie before returning to her eyes. 'Appreciated,' he murmured, a sexy tilt to his full mouth.

Swallowing against the slight constriction of the collar, Tiffany lowered her gaze to the table and the job at hand, and for long moments, there was only the quiet click of chips as they stacked and sorted.

Externally anyway. Internally, the throb of her body was a drum beat through her ears as blood washed thick and hot through her system.

'I can do this,' she said, dismissing him as her trembling hands accidentally knocked over a tower of chips. 'You don't need to help.' If anything, the man was a walking, talking – or not, as the case might be – hindrance.

'I know.'

But he didn't stop. He just kept clicking and stacking, the

growing silence shredding Tiffany's last nerve until finally he cleared his throat and said, 'I didn't realise you would be wearing a uniform tonight.'

Her fingers stilled as she glanced his way. 'Oh, sorry... I just assumed you wanted the whole casino vibe? You'd prefer I didn't?'

A half laugh rumbled from his lips. 'It's just very...'

His eyes lifted, taking a slow inspection of her vest from the straps on her shoulders to the row of buttons ending just under her breasts. To what felt like each and every pinstripe on her blouse to the knot of her tie. Goosebumps erupted in its wake, almost as if he'd reached across and trailed his fingers over her skin.

When their eyes met again, he said, 'Distracting.'

Tiffany swallowed, the hammer of her pulse just above the constriction of her collar pronounced, and she itched to pull the knot loose, undo the button, so she could breathe. But she didn't seem to be able to move and she was aware all over again that it was just the two of them in the saloon. Her brain was sending frantic signals to her mouth to say something, to diffuse the situation, but sadly, she wanted to do other things with her mouth right now.

Her body was back in that hotel room where his eyes had raked over her just as thoroughly as they were now.

Except she'd been naked at the time.

She'd relived that night a thousand times these past five months, and the heated memories of his kiss, of his touch, buzzed through her system now with such visceral intensity they activated all her *on* switches. Boss or not, off the clock or not, best friends BIL or not – Tiffany was lit with desire.

Which was not good.

Neither of them were sorting chips any more; they were just

staring at each other. Also, not good. Idle hands and all that. What had he been saying again?

Right... the uniform. Distracting. 'That's kinda the point,' she murmured. 'Of the uniform.'

A slight frown creased his brow momentarily, like he'd also lost track of the conversation before picking up the thread again. He looked her over one more time. 'Yeah.'

'Keep the punters at the table with charms and smiles,' Tiffany reiterated, even though she clearly didn't need to explain casino psychology to a guy who'd probably signed the purchase orders for this very uniform.

Or was certainly the boss of the person who had, anyway.

'Yeah,' he repeated. 'I think...'

Tiffany waited for him to finish, but Theo just let the sentence trail off. 'What do you think?' she pressed, desperate for any conversation to distract her from the staring.

'Maybe we should rethink the uniform.'

It was Tiffany's turn to be puzzled. The uniforms clearly did what they were supposed to do – keep gamblers gambling. Including the male croupier uniforms, which were so slim fitting they might as well have had Velcro fasteners on the shirts and trousers.

Changing that seemed like a dumb business move.

'Why?'

'We want to attract punters, not make them forget why they'd sat down in the first place. Because trust me.' His eyes took another quick tour over her blouse, his gaze roaming hot before it returned to her face. 'You in that uniform? I'm not thinking about gambling at all.'

His gaze locked on hers. 'What are you thinking about?'

It was out before she could stop it. *Stupid*. So stupid. Playing with fire as her libido and the thick pulse between her legs drove her mouth. She had no business asking him such a loaded question. She should have ordered him out of the saloon, or taken him up on his offer to clean up in the morning.

They should be anywhere else but here – alone.

'Trust me,' he said on a harsh huff of air, his eyes holding her captive. 'You don't want to know what I'm thinking.'

Tiffany's breath hitched at the gravel in his voice, which had thickened his accent. Maybe she shouldn't want to – but she did. She sure as shit couldn't think about anything else, and maybe she was playing with fire but her chin lifted anyway. 'Maybe I do.'

His lips quirked in a slight smile. 'It's... not exactly suitable for work.'

'Just as well I'm off the clock, then.' Now she was definitely playing with fire. 'I'm a big girl, Theo. Why don't you let me decide what I can handle in my down time?'

Blue eyes locked on hers as he picked up his glass and took a slug of whisky, watching her over the rim as he swallowed. Holding her gaze, he brought it back to the table but held it firm. 'I want to strip off your tie, rip open the buttons of your blouse, push up your skirt, bend you over this table and fuck you from behind.'

Tiffany's heart banged hard against her ribs as each filthy word dropped like stones into the silence. She supposed she was meant to recoil from his deliberate crudity. Be shocked. Scandalised. Affronted.

It would have been a lot easier if she was.

But she wasn't. She was titillated. Her breath roughened with every detail as he took her right into the thick of the fantasy until she was picturing herself, stiletto-clad feet wide apart, legs spread as if he was frisking her instead of fucking her, her lacy bra exposed as his big body surrounded her, fully dressed apart from his open fly as he pounded her all the way to the climax she could already feel simmering between her legs.

Jesus. She shouldn't want that. But she did. The throb between her legs intensified as a husky breath slid slowly from her lips. 'A shame about that no-sex dare, huh?'

And the fact she had more self-respect than being a rich man's plaything.

The angle of his jaw clenched white as he raised his glass to her, his lips twisting into an ironic smile as he drank, draining the remains in one swallow. It thudded as it landed on the table.

'Maybe don't wear the uniform tomorrow night,' he said, then turned away throwing, 'Goodnight, Tiffany, sweet dreams,' over his shoulder like he hadn't just almost brought her to orgasm from words alone.

Sweet dreams? Fat chance of that.

* * *

Theo stopped at the saloon entrance the next night. Tiffany was behind the tables again, dispersing chips. In her uniform. Looking as sexy and untouchable as the previous night, the neat knot of her tie taunting him, her Robert-Palmer-glossy lipstick beckoning like a siren from the rocks.

As if she sensed his presence, she glanced up from the chips and their gazes locked. For a beat, she didn't look so sure of herself, before the uncertainty vanished and she smiled at him, a very definite challenge in her eyes. 'Evening, Tiffany,' he murmured.

'Evening, boss.' She returned the greeting with an irritating amount of chirpiness.

'Hey, boss,' Kelly said, oblivious to the undercurrent. 'The others close behind? I've mixed together a signature cocktail to start the night but won't pour if they're a while away.'

'They should be here in a few minutes,' he replied as he crossed casually to the back of the room where the tables were set up.

'Awesome. I'll get them out on a tray now.'

Coming to a halt in front of her, Theo lowered his voice. 'I thought we agreed you weren't going to wear the croupier uniform any more?'

It had starred in his dreams last night. Fevered dreams that had woken him this morning in a twist of sheets with raging morning wood that wouldn't quit. Not until he took himself in hand and did something about it while picturing the exact filthy scenario he had laid out to her last night.

That he wanted to do – for real – right now. Ask Kelly to leave, lock the door and fuck her over the blackjack table.

Flicking a glance over his shoulder at Kelly, Tiffany also kept her voice low. 'I don't think *we* agreed to anything.'

'*Theé dóse mou dýnamierde*,' Theo muttered under his breath, asking for strength.

Her and that fucking uniform was going to be the death of him. How was he supposed to concentrate on gambling when he wanted to pop all those buttons and bury his face in her tits?

'What if I asked you nicely?'

'I'd ask you if that was an order.'

Christe. An order. Do not think about ordering her out of that uniform. Ordering her to her knees. Ordering her to open her plush, red mouth. 'What if I said yes?'

'I would say, "But sir, I'd be disappointing your guests, who don't seem to have a problem with what I'm wearing."'

Theo snorted. Of course they fucking didn't. They were guys with twenty-twenty vision. Even Hugo had joked this afternoon that she could turn him straight when she'd found some aloe vera ointment for his nasty sunburn.

Which had made Theo irrationally pissed off.

Watching his so-called friends flirting with her all day because they knew how it annoyed him was making him crazy. Hell, they'd be merciless if they knew he and Tiffany had already slept together.

Theo narrowed his eyes. 'I can live with their disappointment.'

Separating the chips into piles, she said, 'What if I was to tell you I like it? It's *boss*. I like how flattering it is to all these big bones of mine. And yes' – she lifted her gaze and caught his eye – 'I like the way men look at me in it.'

Her gaze held a clear you-got-a-problem-with-that? challenge. And he didn't. The uniform flattered her Rubenesque form perfectly, and the fact she knew that and got off on the attention it brought her was sexy AF.

But conversely, it also made him want to break things.

'I *don't* like the way men look at you in it.' And yeah, that might make him a Neanderthal, but he could live with that, too.

She smiled sweetly then returned her attention to the chips. 'I guess that's a you problem.'

Narrowing his eyes, he leaned in as he murmured, 'You know this is playing with fire. You know where this is going to lead?' Theo never considered himself much of a sage, but there was an inevitability about them that both scared and attracted him in equal measure.

'Yeah, except' – she looked up again and also leaned in a little – 'I wasn't stupid enough to take a no-sex vow.' She straightened and returned her attention to the chips.

Well, she had him there.

9

The rest of the week followed pretty much the same pattern as the first day. Theo driving the boat around islands, stopping here and there as the whim took them. Water sports, swimming, beer drinking, tenders taken into island villages, freshly caught and cooked seafood bought straight from fisherman plying their catch from their berths in stone-walled harbours.

And in the evenings, his daily dose of torture thanks to Tiffany and that uniform.

He'd seen her during the day of course, serving drinks and meals and being friendly and chatty with the guys, usually about Australia and her family cattle station in the Top End – as it was apparently known.

They loved her, a fact they never tired of telling him.

And as far as crew went, she was exceptionally good. Efficient, friendly, no drama. Fitting in with not just his guests but the crew, who also loved her and never tired of telling him, either. But it was evening Tiffany that had him tossing and turning in his sheets every night. Sexy, bossy, in charge. Running the tables with a strict decorum but always with a sassy flash of her red lips and that wicked sense of humour.

Goading, charming, daring them to part with their chips.

Until finally the last night which, frankly, despite the good times this past week catching up with his old friends, Theo had been looking forward to, far too much. Only one more session with Tiffany in that uniform.

He might actually manage to keep his sanity intact.

Because it was their last night on the boat – and probably because Theo just wanted it over and done with – the guys were apparently indefatigable, and by the time he ordered their drunk and comically disorderly asses out of his saloon at almost two in the morning, he was unaccountably twitchy. There was an itch in his blood and a tension in his muscles and a throb in his groin that made him want to peel his skin off.

Partly because, unlike his friends, he'd barely had anything to drink. Mostly because tonight, instead of keeping eye contact with him to a minimum, Tiffany had side-eyed him so often it was a wonder she hadn't developed a nystagmus.

Which was the tuxedo's fault.

When Fabian had suggested a few days back that they should have some tuxedos delivered to the boat and wear them for their last casino night to surprise Tiffany, it had seemed like a fun idea and the guys had been all in.

And she *had* been surprised.

In fact, she'd gaped as they'd sauntered into the saloon in their black pants and black jackets complete with black satin lapel, snowy-white shirts and black bowties. Then she'd laughed, inspecting each man and nodding with approval, dropping a quip about being in the presence of the Rat Pack.

But then her gaze landed on him and it seemed like the dumbest idea in the history of dumb ideas. Because there'd been no brisk approval, no quick quip. Just the parting of that red mouth and the cling of her gaze as it had lingered over the contours of his tux. From the broad cut of his shoulders down to the tips of his shiny black leather shoes.

And up again.

In that instant Theo's entire world narrowed down to the thorough caress of her gaze. The noise and chatter of the guys helping themselves to drinks had receded as the tempo of his heartbeat, a slow thud in his ears, had taken over.

When her eyes had returned to his, Theo had seen the same hunger in her gaze he'd seen the night of the wedding. When he'd also been wearing a tux.

But she'd merely said, 'Don't scrub up too badly there, boss,' as she'd pulled her gaze off him to the activity at the bar and asked, 'Who wants to lose their money first?'

Unanimously, the guys had nominated Fabian and laughter filled the saloon, breaking Theo out of his daze, his surroundings coming back into sharp focus again, his body systems coming back online. Air had rushed in and out of his lungs, his legs had solidified beneath him and, consciously, he'd slipped his business mask on because it was going to be the only way he'd remember that Tiffany *fucking* Wainwright was totally off limits.

And he'd needed it every time her hazel gaze had strayed in his direction.

Unlike other nights, she hadn't rationed her interactions with him, hadn't kept a tight rein on how many times she looked at him. Sure, they may have only been brief lapses, but every single one of them had left sticky fingerprints all over his libido.

And now here they were. Alone again. His one-and-done rule and that fucking no-sex dare doing little to cool the fever running though his blood.

Would Ari know if he broke it? No. But Theo would know...

'I'm sorry about keeping you up so late,' he murmured as he headed for the bar and the whisky like he'd done that first time but not since.

Because he hadn't wanted to put himself in the path of temptation.

Tonight, though, he wasn't feeling rational. He owned this goddamned boat – he could sit in this bar all fucking night if he wanted. Of course, he should not do that. He should not have the drink he was pouring. He should not do anything other than get his ass to bed.

But the path to temptation was littered with should nots.

'I don't mind.'

Her voice was quiet and stilted and Theo glanced in her direction to find her head down, sorting chips, stacking methodically, denying him eye contact, denying him the hunger he knew still lurked in her pragmatic hazel eyes. And it felt like a spike was being driven into the base of his skull because he wanted her to look at him, he wanted to see that hunger again now they were alone.

Even if he couldn't touch. Even if he could only look.

Taking a sip of his drink, he lounged against the bar as he'd done that first night, arms spread akimbo, the glass dangling from his fingers as *Tiffany's* fingers sorted and stacked. Sorted and stacked. Sorted and stacked.

They were quick and nimble, obviously accomplished at the activity. As accomplished as they'd been at other activities that had created havoc across his body. His belly heated at the memories and he was instantly annoyed at his lack of control where she was concerned, the nail driving in a little further.

'Just leave them,' he said testily. 'Go to bed. It's late and the equipment doesn't have to be returned until tomorrow after-noon. You're officially off the clock.'

Her chin lifted and she pierced him with a haughty glare. 'I'm a grown adult, Theo. I decide when I go to bed, not you.' The frost in her voice belied the fire in her eyes. 'It's stacking chips, not digging ditches. It's hardly difficult. And it's part of my goddamned job. On or off the clock, I'll leave when it's done.'

Theo blinked at her outburst. Was this tension between them getting to her, too?

If he'd been another kind of boss, he could have chided her over her insubordination or for defying a direct order, but he was too busy revelling in the fire that had flared like brimstone in her eyes.

Fire that lit an answering flare in his body, licking heat to every inch.

He held up his palms in a *do as you like* gesture, and she got back to the task, the blur of her fingers and the clink of chips keeping him company as he sipped his whiskey.

'Must you watch?' she asked after a minute, interrupting the wild churn of his thoughts.

She didn't look up from the table, but the thick thread of exasperation in her voice was clear. Theo almost laughed. Her question implied he had some control over this thing when he decidedly did not. He couldn't *not* look at her. But he wasn't about to admit to that, so he settled for answering her question with another.

'Can I help?' He hadn't asked last time but her mood hadn't been so hostile and the tension between them hadn't been as thick and knotted as it was now after six nights of this tango. 'Two hands are faster than one, right?'

Her head snapped up, her eyes flashed. 'Why don't you go to bed?'

Theo, unperturbed by her irritation, shrugged. 'Not tired.' Which probably made him sound like a petulant child, but he knew another long night of thinking about her in that uniform awaited him and if he was going to be haunted by it, he'd rather see the real thing.

Finishing his whisky, he straightened and half turned to pour himself a second, adding three fingers to the glass before sliding the stopper into the neck of the decanter. Taking a sip, he placed the tumbler on the bar then shrugged out of his jacket and threw it around the back of a high-backed stool. Between the fever in his blood and the brimstone in her eyes, he was too damn hot for a jacket.

When he glanced at Tiffany again, she hadn't returned to her chip sorting. She was just standing there, her eyes roving over his chest like she was trying to decide where might be a good place to take a bite.

And fuck if that didn't feel like a sledgehammer to his dick.

There was nothing for it now as the devil took hold. The frankness of her gaze only made him hotter and there was no way was he stopping at his jacket. Casually, he reached for his bowtie and pulled on a tail, a surge of very male satisfaction flaring through his body as her eyes bugged.

'What are you doing?' she asked, her voice a breathy thread of air suspended between them.

The entire bow came undone with that one movement and he left the tails hanging down to look all James Bond and badass as he reached for the top button of his shirt. It felt like a noose around his neck as a well of desire flushed from his groin to his belly to his chest, surging like a tsunami to flood his throat.

'It's hot in here, don't you think?'

'No.' She shook her head as her gaze fell to the twist of his fingers.

The button popped and he huffed out a breath. Her eyes were hot on his throat as he stretched his neck from side to side. 'That's better,' he murmured.

Then he started on his cuffs.

Her eyes rounded again as she tracked the movement and Theo's body pulled taut as a bow. He wasn't sure what the game plan was here; maybe it was just a tease to counteract the prolonged torment of that indecent uniform. But he sure as fuck wasn't going to stop.

He couldn't stop.

Not when his pulse thrummed through his body and her intense focus on his every action constricted his breath and throbbed through his balls, making him hyperaware of how good they'd been together and how long it had been since they'd burned up the sheets.

Had he been a monk in that time? Nope. Not until the celibacy thing, anyway. But no woman he'd been with since – or before – had held him in such thrall.

The silence built as the buttons on his cuffs ceded to his fingers, and he rolled his sleeves to mid-forearm, watching her watch him the entire time. And Theo made damn sure he put on a show, not rushing it, conscious of Tiffany's gaze glued to every minute twitch of his fingers and turn of his wrist.

She glared at him with stormy eyes when he was finally done, his arms folded. 'You did that deliberately.'

Theo smiled at her red-lipped outrage. 'I have no idea what you're talking about.'

Which was a grave mistake. Because now that his very PG baring of minimal flesh was done, the sudden glitter in her eyes told him she did not appreciate being manipulated.

And she knew how to hit back.

Moving out from behind the table, she walked towards him in a manner he could best describe as deliberately provocative. She didn't stop until she was close enough for him to reach out and touch, but the sparks arcing from her body warned that she'd eviscerate him if he did.

Some men apparently found it hard to read women. Theo never had. He certainly had zero problems reading the hostility and frustration burning in Tiffany's eyes.

She held there for a beat before lifting her hand to her bowtie and pulling on the tail, causing it to unravel much like his, the scrap of fabric hanging loose around her neck. But she didn't stop there, pulling on one side until it came free from her collar, and Theo swore that the zipping sound of fabric sliding against fabric in the utter stillness of the room was the sexual equivalent of a woman shaking her hair loose from an up-do.

Or taking off her glasses.

The pièce de résistance was her tossing the unravelled fabric on the ground like it was something she did every night as she stripped for bed.

Christe!

She might as well have ripped open her blouse for the immediate chain reaction it set in motion. His pulse surged on a roar that reverberated through his entire circulatory system, diverting blood to his cock so swiftly, the erection almost brought Theo to his knees.

'You're right,' she said with that Mona Lisa smile of hers. 'Much better.'

If he thought that was it, he was wrong. She was not done toying with him yet as her eyes undertook a thorough inspection of his body, raking from the crown of his head to the tips of his shoes.

Yep. She'd definitely turned the tables.

For a few minutes when he'd removed his tie and rolled up his sleeves, Theo had held her in the palm of his hand, but by being smug, he'd created a monster. And now it was he, suspended in a web of sexual torment, waiting with bated breath on her next move.

Just as soon as she'd looked her fill, obviously.

'Oh,' she murmured, glancing up from his feet. 'Your lace is undone.'

Theo, still reliving the unwrapping of the bowtie on a loop in his brain, frowned. Looking down, he confirmed the situation. About to shrug it off, he stopped as she took a step closer. A step so close, the fan of her warm breath brushed his chin as the height of her stilettos brought their mouths to within kissing distance.

Then she slowly but surely started to drop, and Theo swore he felt that breath brush everything in a straight line from the ridge of his throat to the tight bunch of his quads.

His chest, his abs, his cock. His very hard cock, which must be patently fucking obvious now she was fully crouched in front of him.

Expelling a breath, Theo reached for his whisky and took a deep swallow as, head bowed, Tiffany wordlessly reached for the lace and tied it in a double bow. He gripped the glass hard as his pulse slugged hot and urgent through his groin, and he desperately tried not to think about the sexual connotation of their position.

But when she tipped her chin and met his gaze and said through that shiny red mouth, 'Anything else I can do for you while I'm down here, sir?' he knew he was fucked.

He might have started this, but she was going to finish it.

Dredging resistance from God knew where, he gave her a sardonic smile. 'Thank you, stew, that won't be necessary.'

'Are you sure?' One of those thickly arched brows of hers winged upwards as she reached for his belt. 'You look kinda tense. I probably have' – she pursed her red pouty mouth briefly before continuing – 'just the thing for that.'

Her blatant suggestion was like a direct squeeze to his balls and Theo almost groaned out loud. 'Tiffany,' he warned, his pulse a hammer at his temples.

'After all,' she reminded him again as her fingers pulled the belt free of its loop and went to work on the buckle, 'I didn't take any celibacy vow.'

Like he needed to be reminded of that. 'Tiffany,' he muttered as she made short work of the buckle. 'This is not appropriate.'

Her hand stilled on the button of his waistband. 'You want me to stop?'

She looked at him through lashes liberally plied in mascara, her smoky kohled eyes all big and round and innocent. Despite the taut spiral of tension cramping every muscle, Theo gave a grudging smile. How was it possible to look so damn virtuous with that red mouth hinting at something so fucking wicked?

'I don't want you to... service me like it's part of your job description.'

The words spilled out harsher than he'd meant, but they were as much for him as they were for her. With very little blood left in his brain, he was finding resistance harder and harder and, as a guy who was usually well disciplined, it was discombobulating.

He'd certainly never lost his head like this with a woman. Breaching God knew how many employer conduct codes and workplace laws, not to mention dicing a little too close to the edge with the whole celibacy thing. He should reach down and yank her to her feet, but that mouth of hers ratcheted up his level of thrall.

'But what if I want to service you?' She met his gaze directly as her fingers worked to undo the button of his fly.

Theo swallowed. The way she said service was *in*-fucking-*decent*.

'What if I get off on making a hot Greek playboy billionaire look at me like that?'

The button popped.

'Like what?' he asked, his breath roughening as Tiffany slowly lowered the zip, the metallic scrape of the pull tab and the teeth opening – one by fucking one – like a fingernail scraping along his shaft. 'How am I looking at you?'

'Like I created the heavens and earth and that you'd give anything' – the zip reached the bottom – 'the contents of your bank account, this boat, your next breath, for me to open my mouth and take your cock.' Her hand slipped away as her hazel gaze pinned him to the spot. 'Right. To. The. Back.'

Theo felt every word that spilled from those plush red lips as if she'd licked them into the flesh slung low between his hip bones while she looked up at him through those eyelashes. The urge to thrust his fingers into her hair, to rub his thumb over those filthy, filthy lips was so overwhelming, he shoved the hand not holding his glass into his pocket.

The silence in the saloon was absolute as neither moved. They just stared at each other – him looking down, her looking up. Him with his trousers open, her crouched in her high heels. But *not* in supplication. In full control.

Several beats passed, the thud of his heart marking each one until, finally, she rose to her feet, took the glass from his hand and downed the contents in one swallow.

'On second thoughts,' she said, slipping the tumbler onto the bar behind, 'I think I will leave clean up till the morning.'

Then, cool as you fucking please, she turned on her heel and sashayed out of the saloon throwing, 'Sweet dreams, Theo,' over her shoulder as she exited.

Which he totally deserved.

On second thought, she'd skipped the cab, for her the car behind, "I think I've seen one of the morning." Then cool as you liked or please the moment for a man, pushed out of the when the vest, swear it was a. Theo over her shoulder as she called.

Which he really deserved.

10

Tiffany spent the next fortnight on the boat trying to have as little contact with Theo as possible. She'd gone to bed that night, her legs so wobbly it was a wonder she hadn't broken her goddamn ankle in those stilettos, and even now two weeks later, she couldn't believe her audacity.

Her bravado.

Considering he'd already confessed what he'd wanted to do to her in her uniform, she'd been playing with fire. But when he'd walked in with that tux fitting him like the gods on Mount Olympus had tailored it especially for him, looking as sexy as he had that night he had blown her brain at Ari and Kelsey's wedding, it had put her straight back in his bed.

Or the hotel bed, anyway.

Which had only stoked the slow burn of having his eyes on her all week – on her mouth, on her bowtie, on the way her breasts were framed by the vest. Then he'd shrugged out of his jacket and her body had lit up, and he'd known it, which had made her cranky and irritable, but that hadn't stopped him from his little strip tease. If anything, it had encouraged him.

Cocky Greek bastard.

And she'd been powerless to resist the show as he'd pulled on his bowtie and slowly rolled up the snowy cotton cuffs of his sleeves like he'd invented forearm porn.

Thank God for that smug, triumphant expression he'd been wearing all over his face at the conclusion or she might really have done something stupid. Like challenge him to a game of strip poker until they were both naked and he did fuck her over the blackjack table despite all the reasons they shouldn't.

Not least because he was her boss.

Yeah, that look had drilled into her brain and hit a major nerve, her knee-jerk reaction not exactly well thought out, but the point had been made. Sure, she was hot for him, but he wasn't exactly immune to her either and she could bring him to his knees with relative ease.

Something they both seemed to silently acknowledge these past two weeks as they went about their business, interacting when required but keeping it to the barest of minimums. Which, logistically, hadn't been that difficult.

They'd been docked at Flisvos Marina on the Athens waterfront since they'd dropped off five very happy Englishmen and Theo had spent a lot of his days attending to business. A lot of meetings and appointments saw him coming and going, sometimes even spending the night in his downtown apartment rather than returning to the boat.

Tiffany tried not to think about if or who he might be entertaining in his apartment because it was none of her business. But the thoughts sometimes crept in anyway, sitting very uncomfortably in the pit of her stomach. Sure, Theo had seemed determined to stick to the celibacy route, but there was a helluva lot of fooling around that could be done, which would technically not see him in breach of the dare he'd made to Ari.

Like, if she had blown him in the saloon, strictly speaking, there would have been zero sex involved, right?

And if he'd stuck to the dare for the last two months, then he was probably more than ready to succumb to temptation. Especially after the rather prolonged tease of the week his guests were on the *Nerida*.

But as tempted as she was to see if Theo had been papped somewhere in Athens, she did not google his name. She had to remember at the end of the day he was Theo Callisthenes, Greek tycoon/playboy who owned a superyacht and had made sleeping around an art form. And she was second stew on said yacht who, yes, had slept with him one amazing night, but who now slept below deck, in a single bunk.

And if that didn't bring it right back to basics, she didn't know what did.

Yes, it had been fun – incredible, actually – but they were done. Even if their chemistry still zipped and sparkled and she truly believed he felt it too, she had no desire to be a rich man's plaything. Available at Theo's whim like his bloody superyacht. Taking it out at his convenience then leaving it in the dock when he preferred more land-based pursuits.

Tiffany wasn't dumb enough to set her heart on a guy who'd never been in a romantic relationship. Ever. Or who clearly had a wandering eye. She was not her mother.

So she'd kept her head down and attended to what little chores there were on the stationary boat. Occasionally she went into Athens, sometimes by herself to explore, sometimes with the others, usually for lunch somewhere. Once, she'd even met Kelsey, who was in the city overnight before she and her mother flew to London to see an eye specialist.

Her bestie had pumped her for all the juicy details about life on board the *Nerida* with Theo, but Tiffany had been unusually reticent about spilling any info. Largely because she didn't want to encourage Kelsey's fever dream about besties getting all wifed up with brothers. But also because talking about it made it a thing. And it was not a thing.

No matter how much Kelsey was rooting for it.

Mostly though, there was an enormous amount of free time. Tiffany didn't understand why Theo didn't just lock up the boat and call the staff back if and when he needed them, but she supposed when you had more money than God you could do that kind of thing.

She suspected it also said a lot about his life preferences. It had been evident when they'd talked about his childhood growing up around islands and fishing boats that his love for the sea was ingrained, and although she'd never seen him anywhere other than a wedding and on the *Nerida*, she wondered if, deep down, it was a boat rather than a boardroom where he was most at home.

Not that she or anyone else was complaining. They were being paid well to keep a moored boat – that was used more by them than the owner – shipshape, so if Theo didn't care, why should she? Especially when it gave her oodles of opportunity to work on her book.

She used the days to plot and plan and the nights to write, taking her laptop up to the sky deck in the evenings once the sun had sunk beneath the hills of Athens, taking some of the heat with it. At that time of day, the sky was lit with tangerine and pink and streaked with clouds gilded in rose-gold and, with the *Nerida* moored in such a way that the stern was facing the open sea, she had a front row seat to the glory.

The rest of the crew tended to go indoors after dinner, retiring to the media room to watch a movie on the big-screen television, so she usually had the deck to herself, which she loved. Up here she could sit cross-legged on a sun lounger and let the musings of the day percolate from her brain and out through her fingertips as the sky changed from dusk to twilight to night.

The recent island-hopping with Theo's British friends had given her endless descriptive fodder for scenery, and her mind swirled with the vivid colours of her book as she rushed to get it all down. Breathing life into the watery world of Astraon – where the stars shone from the ocean floor and mermaids, not moons, controlled the tides – was exciting and exhausting in equal measure, but weaving this tale that had been living in her head since she'd been a girl also felt necessary.

And Tiffany was pleased with her progress, time flying every night as her fingers tippy-tapped over the keyboard, until the pressure of words eased and she was spent. Only then did she look up to find a hush had fallen over the marina and it was just her and the stars, although with all the light pollution from Athens, she could see precious few of them.

It was usually about now, as she was finishing up for the night, she heard Theo come on board – if he was spending the night on the yacht. He never made much noise, but it was so quiet this late she could often hear the plaintive meow of the marina cat as it prowled around. Her whole body would tense as she strained to hear his footfalls, wondering if he'd seek her out. Wondering if he even knew she was up here.

He never had – phew! – and, as far as she knew, he went straight to his suite, but just knowing he was on the *Nerida* caused a frisson of awareness that followed her all the way to her bunk and into her dreams.

Sighing, she closed her laptop lid and reclined on the lounge a little, adjusting the messy topknot she'd shoved her hair in earlier a little higher. She inhaled the still warm air. It smelled of salt and sea and the faintest whiff of the damp seaweed that gathered around the waterline of the harbour wall, and she felt at peace and so grateful and lucky to be able to call somewhere this beautiful home.

For now, anyway.

It was so far removed from where she came from, she had to pinch herself sometimes even if she did miss Balmain Downs where the aromas were very different. Dust and cattle. Hay and leather. Eucalyptus and petrichor. And the night skies were next level. No light pollution out there where stars hung in the outback sky like crystal diamantes dripping from chandeliers and the cloudy shimmer of the Milky Way shone vibrantly luminescent, like thousands of glow worms in the night.

But she hadn't missed seeing her father every day. Or the tension between the two of them, never far from the surface. Or the resentment from her brothers, who she loved but who didn't understand why she couldn't just *get over it*. Get over her father making her complicit in his infidelity and forever poisoning Tiffany's relationship with her mother. Get over letting Mikey leave without any support or safety net because he wanted to make art and love men, not wrangle cattle and eat dust all his life.

They'd hated how the strained father-daughter relationship often blew up at the worst possible time and, in the end, it had been a relief for everyone – including her – when she'd walked away.

The faint sound of footsteps and low distant murmur of a voice somewhere in the marina drifted to her on the night air, and Tiffany tuned into it for a beat or two. It grew closer and closer until she realised it was Theo on his phone, his low laughter carrying towards her like a hug on the warm air as he stepped onto the cast rail of the *Nerida*.

With zero shame, she eavesdropped on his conversation that was now coming from below on the main deck aft. Not that she could understand a word given it was all in Greek. Well, she got 'mama' and 'baba', which she knew to be mum and dad, and occasionally he mentioned Ari, once even Kelsey, but that was the extent of what she could translate.

As much as she could tell, he didn't seem to be moving around, his voice coming from the one direction, and Tiffany pictured him lounging against the back rail as he chatted, his legs thrust out in front, his shorts riding up a little, the dark hair of his quads and calves emphasising the superb musculature of his legs.

He really did have the most amazing legs. And chest. And ass. Not to mention that lethal weapon between his legs which he'd used to thoroughly shock and awe. Thoughts of that made her squirm in her chair, yanking her out of the trip down memory lane.

Bloody hell, woman. Do not think about Theo's junk!

Dragging her mind out of Theo's underwear, she tuned back into the conversation just in time to hear him say, '*Kalinyhta*,' which Tiffany knew was goodnight.

There was silence then and she supposed he'd be heading to bed. And so should she. She'd just wait for five to make sure the coast was clear. Which sounded like a great plan until ten seconds later she heard footsteps coming up the closest stairs and she knew he was heading for the sky deck.

For a panicked moment her eyes darted around, looking for somewhere to hide. Behind the bar? In the shadows down by the jacuzzi? Under her sun lounger? Which were all crazy and also moot as he stepped onto the deck before she had a chance to move a muscle.

In a suit.

'Oh, hey.' He pulled up short, clearly taken aback at her presence. 'I'm sorry. I didn't know you were up here.'

Tiffany blinked. 'It's fine.' The man didn't need to apologise for walking around his own damn boat.

If he needed to apologise for anything it was how sinfully well he wore a suit. He hadn't been wearing that when he'd left this morning so she could only presume he'd come from a late meeting and hadn't bothered with changing his clothes.

The trousers with a faint burgundy pin-stripe had been tailored to cling to quads and narrow hips and cup that bulge she'd been trying not to think about as if he was wearing Lycra bicycle shorts. His shirt was white, sitting flat against his belly and open at the neck, the top two buttons undone like he'd removed a tie at some point. The matching jacket encased his shoulders, not only emphasising their breadth but somehow managing to draw attention to his entire physique.

Like a gilt frame around a famous painting.

Rousing herself from her inappropriate – which seemed to be their thing – inspection, Tiffany cleared her throat and swung her legs over the edge of the lounge. 'I'll... go.'

'No, no.' He waved her back. 'Please. I don't want to chase you away. Ari and I just closed a big deal for two new ships and I'm a little wired.' He laughed, clearly very happy at the outcome. 'Also' – his lips quirked conspiratorially – 'I might have had one or two ouzos to celebrate.'

Tiffany's breath hitched at how dashingly devilish he looked in the night, high on shots and his boardroom win, his hair falling haphazardly against his forehead, a grin tugging at his mouth. This uninhibited version of Theo should send her scurrying to her cabin – immediately – but he reminded her too much of the Theo she'd first met at the wedding. The charming, champagne-offering guy who had nothing more pressing in his life than seduction.

And that, for good or for ill, kept her ass planted on the lounge. 'Congratulations,' she said with a smile.

'Thanks. Ari got an excellent deal and our fleet is now two ships stronger.'

Tiffany had thought their first serious interaction after their boundary pushing two weeks ago would be awkward AF, but it wasn't. His triumph was infectious. She quirked an eyebrow. 'World domination, huh?'

He threw back his head and laughed, drawing her gaze to the bronzed column of his throat. This morning, as had been his routine since heading into Athens every day, his face had been cleanly shaven. Just over twelve hours later, dark shadow had replaced the smooth contours of his jaw, and she shivered remembering how good his five o'clock shadow had felt on the inside of her thighs.

'We're expanding our offerings into the Caribbean market,' he supplied when his laughter had eased.

'Are the ships sea ready?'

'No.' He shook his head as he crossed to the side of the boat nearest her, leaning his ass against the solid edge. 'Full refits in Ōceanós branding first. They should both be ready for passengers this time next year.'

Tiffany whistled. 'That sounds expensive.'

'It is.' He grinned, like hundreds of millions of dollars was nothing. Folding his arms, he tipped his chin at her laptop. 'You're writing?'

'Yeah.' She nodded. 'I've been coming up here most nights since we've been moored. It's peaceful, and being able to look up from my keyboard and see the ocean is really great for inspiration.'

'Yeah.' He turned, placing his hands on the curved mould-ing, and stared out at the shifting mass of calm water. 'Even at night, there's this force to it that just sort of wells up through your feet and lodges in your throat.'

Tiffany blinked at his almost poetic observation. 'Maybe you should be the writer,' she murmured.

Laughing, Theo turned. 'Ouzo goggles. Although' – he absently rubbed his jawline, and Tiffany swore she could feel the faint scrape of new stubble right between her legs – 'my mother did just tell me on the phone that my father wrote to her every day for a year when they were first in love and she still has them, and it's their thirtieth wedding anniversary today so maybe it runs in the family.'

So he'd been speaking to his mother.

Tiffany had first met Theo's parents not long after Kelsey and Ari had got together, and a couple of times after that. Then at the wedding, of course. They were gracious and welcoming and both clearly still besotted with each other, laughing at each other's jokes, finishing sentences, holding hands, their heads often bent together in private conversation.

Watching them together, she'd been envious of their close-ness and longevity. Tiffany supposed having money eased a lot of potential flash points in a relationship, but her parents had been well off – not Callisthenes rich but not wanting for much either – and that hadn't made things easier for them.

'They're lucky,' she said. 'You're lucky.'

11

The words sounded a little bitter and Tiffany instantly wished she could recall them. Theo Callisthenes – her boss – did not need to know about the saga of the Wainwright family. He already knew too much about her as it was, and family stuff was private. Not even Kelsey knew the full story. But given she'd only just been thinking about home, it was hardly surprising she'd be envious.

'I know.' He shoved his hands in his pockets and fixed her with his cool blue eyes. 'I take it your parents don't have a great relationship?'

That was putting it mildly. 'No.' A husky note in her voice betrayed the emotion behind that one simple little word.

'They're divorced?'

'Yes.' She cleared her throat. 'I was fifteen.'

'Tough age.'

She shrugged. In a lot of ways it had been a relief not to have to keep her father's secrets any more; she just hadn't thought her mother would lash out the way she had, accusing Tiffany of collusion. Hadn't been prepared to be so brutally sidelined when the married man who'd slept with half the women in the district had not been.

'You have brothers, right?'

Pleased to be veering away from the topic of her parents, Tiffany nodded. She'd told Rufus a bit about her brothers when he'd asked her about Balmain Downs, which Theo had been present for, and she'd occasionally mentioned them at the table the times they all ate together. 'Four,' she confirmed.

'And you're the youngest?'

'No.' She shook her head. 'Gordy, Mack and Trapper are older by a few years. Mikey is a year younger.'

'And they're all still at home helping to run the ranch?'

Tiffany smiled at the Americanism. 'Station,' she corrected. 'And no. Mikey left home.'

'It wasn't for him?'

The understatement choked a hollow laugh from the depths of her throat. 'Living with a bunch of old-fashioned, He-Man cowboys in the middle of butt-fuck nowhere on a cattle station when you're arty, gay and vegetarian isn't necessarily mutually exclusive, but in Mikey's case it was.'

'Ah.' He nodded. 'Your family weren't... understanding?'

'The family were okay, they were more disturbed about the vegetarian thing to be honest. My dad had a harder time understanding why Mikey wanted to leave. He never understood why anyone would want to live anywhere but the outback.'

Once upon a time, Tiffany had thought that, too.

'They argued about that most of all. He tried to persuade Mikey to stay, offered to build him a studio, but as my brother was fond of saying, sometimes at the top of his lungs, an artist needed to experience life, so in the end he left without my father's blessing or support and predictions that he'd be back with his tail between his legs.'

'And your mother?'

Beverly Wainwright had become Beverly Martin, moving on to a new life as a trophy wife to a man twenty years her senior. 'She was... busy.'

Clearly taking her brevity as a hint, Theo changed the subject. Sort of. 'What kind of artist is he?'

Tiffany's mood brightened instantly. She could rave about Mikey's art all night. 'Landscape,' she said. 'But with a modern twist.'

And then because no matter who asked, Tiffany would always pull out her phone and scroll to examples of her brother's art, she did the same for Theo, pulling up the gallery website of which she was a silent partner.

'This is him.' Leaving her laptop on the sun lounger, she crossed to where Theo was standing and handed over her phone. Their hands accidentally brushed and the familiar prickle of awareness that zapped from his fingertips to hers reminded her not to get too close.

The screen displayed her favourite piece, which hung permanently in the gallery and was not for sale. It was of Balmain Downs, although only very few looking at it would know its exact rural origins. Figures on horseback and cattle were blurred and indistinct, the haze of ochre-red dust being the predominate feature almost sparkling in rays of bright sunshine flooding the canvas.

Tiffany had been on many a muster before the wet season had doused the parched earth, where cattle hooves had kicked up so much dust she could taste it dry and gritty in her mouth and wedged so deeply between her teeth only flossing could remove it.

'This is impressive,' he said, glancing up from the screen.

Tiffany felt the usual swell of pride in her brother at the

compliment and, maybe she was biased, but she agreed whole-heartedly. She was hardly a connoisseur but every cruise ship she'd worked on had its own art gallery that ran auctions, and most of those paintings were nowhere near as good as Mikey's.

Of course, he could just be being polite, because what possible connection could a rich Greek playboy who'd grown up around the sea and boats have to such an arid landscape? But it seemed genuine. 'He's crazy good with light.' Mikey would love the Med, and they'd often talked about him coming over when he got his first big sale. 'If you keep scrolling, you'll see what I mean.'

But he didn't scroll on, he just returned his eyes to the screen. 'Is this what it's like? The Top End?'

'Sometimes.' Tiffany's desire to look at the painting again warred with her need to keep him at a distance but ultimately, she couldn't resist, stepping closer as she turned to plant her ass next to his.

Their arms brushed as she leaned in a little, and goosebumps coursed from her elbow to shoulder blade, but Tiffany's eyes were busy caressing every detail to pay them much heed.

'And then the rains come and everything is lush and green and the creeks flood and the billabongs fill up and the rivers rise and the gum trees flower and the wattles bloom like fluffy bursts of sunshine and it smells fresh and green and lovely.'

'You miss it.'

The heat of his gaze scorched the top of her head. 'Yes,' she murmured, because sometimes she missed it so much it hurt to breathe. 'And no.' Because mostly she really didn't miss all the bloody drama. She turned then to face the sea, resting her bent arms on the edge, a sigh escaping into the sultry Aegean air. 'It's complicated.'

Theo turned too, resting his elbows next to hers. They

weren't touching, but Tiffany was excruciatingly aware of the heat pouring off his body. As if sensing she didn't want to talk about her contradictory answer, Theo scrolled on, the light from the screen illuminating the planes and angles of his face and the way the hollows beneath his cheeks gave way to the granite cut of his jaw.

'Is this a current exhibition?'

'No, he has his own gallery he leases in Sydney. Well, gallery-slash-studio-slash-apartment. He lives upstairs in a cramped flat, paints out the back and has a small area in the front where he displays his art.'

'And does he make a living out of it?'

Tiffany gave a half laugh, thinking about the amount of debt her brother was in. 'Not yet, no. But he will.' She'd never had any doubt about that. 'He's not exactly a starving artist. He makes ends meet. But it's tough getting a toe hold in the art space even if you are insanely talented. Especially if you have to split your focus between creating and selling.'

Add to that a relationship that had cleaned him out and a couple of other bad financial decisions when he'd first high-tailed it to Sydney, and Mikey had been in quite the hole when Tiffany had started working her first cruise ship. He'd been facing down the possibility of fulfilling their father's prophecy of doom and returning home with his tail between his legs and, still angry with her dad, Tiffany hadn't been able to bear the thought.

So she'd offered to help, sinking most of the money she'd earned the past seven years into a gallery that barely broke even.

'Sounds like he needs a benefactor,' Theo mused as he scrolled.

'He has one.'

Of sorts. Maybe that was giving too much away, but she was

proud that she'd been able to help Mikey get back on track. And not just because she knew that one day he'd be a super-rich, super successful artist in his own right but because it would be a big *screw you* to their father.

Immature? Sure. But no less valid.

He didn't say anything for a beat or two but, even looking out into the dark abyss of a moonless sea, Tiffany felt the fan of his gaze like a searchlight on her profile. 'You?'

Lifting her chin, she turned to meet his eye. 'I co-own the gallery, yes.' And she was honoured to be a part of Mikey's artistic enterprise.

'That's very generous of you.'

She shrugged. This was her kid brother; what else was she going to do? 'It's not as glamorous as it sounds.'

He chuckled as he handed back the phone, and Tiffany shivered at the low rumble of air despite the warmth of the night. 'Maybe not but I know how much you earn on a cruise ship.'

It was true; work on a cruise ship wasn't exactly money for jam, but with no food or accommodation costs, no utility bills to pay, no car to upkeep, no need for expensive holidays when every day the ship docked in a different port, outlays were minimal. And a lot of money could be earned in tips.

'But I don't have any real expenses. And I'm hardly going to let Mikey sink when I can help him swim. My father might think that's okay, but I don't.'

A slow smile pulled at the corners of his generous mouth and put a sparkle in his eyes. 'I'm getting the feeling you and your father don't get... on so well?'

Tiffany found herself smiling at his deliberate understatement and at the deftness of his approach. If he'd asked her outright she might have told him to mind his own business, but that smile slipped under her defences. 'You could say that.'

'I'm sorry.'

Tiffany blinked at the unexpected apology. The situation with her father was not his fault, yet there was compassion and empathy in the silky blue depths of his eyes.

'That must be hard,' he continued. 'I'm very close with my father. And it seems like from the little I've gleaned these past few weeks that you were once close to yours, right?'

'Yeah.' She nodded. 'I was.' As she turned back to the ocean, a slight breeze picked up a stray lock of hair that had escaped the up-do and blew across her face. It also wafted a hit of aniseed in her direction. 'And then I walked in on him... in flagrante in a shed with a neighbour's wife when I was twelve and it ripped the blinkers right off my eyes.'

'Tiffany.' It was a hush, a whisper laced with empathy, and she shut her eyes to squeeze back the hot prick of tears. 'I'm sorry you had to see that.'

Her breath got tangled around the lump in her throat. Again with the apologising. She knew this man barely at all compared to her father and yet Theo had apologised to her twice within a few minutes about things that were not of his doing. Unlike her father, who had never apologised for anything that had rippled from that day onwards.

'It probably would have been all right if it had been just that. But he begged me not to tell my mother. He said if nobody knew then nobody could be hurt and that it might break the marriage up, that he'd probably have to leave or that Balmain Downs might even have to be sold and it would be all my fault.'

The brief flattening of his lips in her peripheral vision told Tiffany exactly what Theo thought about her father's emotional blackmail, but he was obviously trying to be measured in his response. 'That was not very nice of him.'

'No, it wasn't.'

Tiffany still remembered the anguish of the time. She remembered the shock of her discovery and the realisation her father was actually just a man like any other, a mere mortal. It had been a bit like when Trapper had told her at the age of six that Santa wasn't real, except multiplied by infinity.

'But I did what he asked. He'd assured me it had been a one-off and ultimately, I couldn't countenance the thought of my mother, of anyone, knowing the truth about my father.' It had been hard enough for her to bear. 'Except I soon realised that Mrs Garrity wasn't the only woman he was screwing. I'd see him with other women at district functions, or he'd be talking at the dinner table about some landowners meeting or other he was going to, or some cattle auction or a business trip to Darwin, and he'd wink at me like I knew what was going on and it was our little secret.'

The sharp twist in her gut was almost as visceral as it had been during those few years she'd been ensnared in her father's web of infidelity, the hot coil of dread like a lead weight in her stomach, and she hadn't realised she'd been wringing her hands until the fingers of his left hand were lacing through the fingers of her right.

So caught up in the past was she, she stared at his long strong fingers for a beat, trying to comprehend why they were there. It was such an unexpected gesture. Not sexual or flirty despite the continued buzz of awareness coursing through her body. It was... comforting. And just what she needed.

'Your mother found out?' he prompted.

'Yes. I don't even know how. But there was an almighty row and, when playing down his sexploits didn't work, he tried to tell her she was overreacting. He told her that I knew about it and didn't have any issues so why should she?'

His thumb set up a soothing tempo rubbing rhythmically along the back of her hand.

'She felt I had betrayed her.'

'You were twelve.' His voice was almost a growl. 'And even if you'd been a fully grown adult, your father's actions were on him, not on you.'

Tiffany shrugged. 'I guess it's easier to lash out and blame someone else than confront the fact your husband couldn't keep his dick in his pants.'

He didn't say anything then, just lifted their joined hands, and Tiffany's gaze snared on him as he pressed a light kiss to her knuckles. It was sweet and made her chest ache and, absurdly, she wanted to turn, she wanted to slide her hands inside his jacket and around his waist and snuggle.

Theo wasn't her boss right now. He was another human being offering comfort.

'She left?' he asked, their eyes meeting, the warmth of his breath playing over her knuckles.

Tiffany nodded. 'She left. And I stayed until I was so resentful people were tiptoeing around us like we were unex-ploded bombs. Then I went travelling and eventually found myself on a cruise ship.'

'And the Top End's loss is our gain.'

She smiled at the wry humour in his tone and part of her wanted to stay up on deck with him for the rest of the night, but she knew she was too emotionally vulnerable right now and she'd probably already told him too much.

'Anyway.' Tiffany disentangled. 'It's late...' They stared at each other for a beat before she smiled and said, 'See you tomorrow.'

He nodded and turned back to the view as she gathered her laptop and departed.

12

Two days later, Theo was twirling in his ergonomically designed chair in his office still thinking about what Tiffany had told him on the sky deck. About where she came from and her brother's art. And her parents and the divorce.

Her father's emotional blackmail. Her mother scapegoating.

Even now, the slow simmer of rage that fizzed to life in his gut wasn't far from boiling over. Tiffany had been twelve. And everything she'd believed about her life had been ripped out from under her. Dark as it had been, he'd seen the devastation in her expression and heard it in her voice. A faint streak of disbelief, like even all these years later, she couldn't comprehend how it had all gone so badly, so quickly.

Sure, in the grand scheme of shitty things that can happen to people, a messy divorce at a pivotal age with parents who'd abdicated the blame onto their kid was very much a first-world problem. But that didn't make the experience of being made piggy in the middle by her parents any less cutting for Tiffany.

Yet she'd somehow managed to put it behind her and become a functioning adult, forging her own way and giving her brother a hand up as well. And he admired the hell out of her for it – more than that, he wanted to make things right for her. Slay her dragons even though she'd proven she was more than capable of her own dragon-slaying.

Tossing the pen he'd been idly twirling, Theo rose and strolled to the windows, shoving his hands in his pockets, clenching his fists as he thought about how much he'd like to plant one square in the middle of Marshall Wainwright's philandering face. Theo may well have slept his way around Europe – and a few other continents – but he'd never put a ring on anyone's finger.

His thoughts slid to Angelika before they slid hastily away.

Fidelity and honour in marriage – as in business – had not only been ingrained by his father and grandfather but it had been all around. Marriage was sacrosanct in the Callisthenes family and he need look no further than his elders to see it on display.

That was not to say that Theo wasn't a realist. He understood that a lot of marriages didn't work out and ended, oftentimes for the better of both parties. And he knew people strayed in relationships for a variety of reasons and that things were rarely black and white, but there were no excuses for crossing any fidelity lines as far as he was concerned.

And for damn sure he took that judgement with him into business dealings.

A man who could screw around on his wife/partner/significant other wouldn't think twice about screwing around on a deal. If he couldn't be trusted to honour the most sacred vow a person could take, then why would Theo ever trust that person in business?

That didn't mean he hadn't done deals with people who'd

failed the honour test. It just meant that contracts were airtight and there was zero wriggle room.

Theo's gaze zoomed over the urban sprawl of the city to the sea, a deep dazzling blue stretching all the way to the horizon, wishing he was there already instead of waiting on this one last meeting. But it freed him up for the next couple of weeks and tomorrow they were setting off to Crete, and he was already impatient to be on board.

It had been too long since the *Nerida* had been out, and using her as a glorified crash pad was an insult to her true purpose in life. And then there was Tiffany. He'd be lying to himself if he didn't admit the thought of seeing her every day for more than a few minutes here and there wasn't just as alluring as time on the water.

Even if putting temptation right in his path was like playing sexual chicken with that ridiculous dare.

'I thought you were gone?'

Theo glanced over his shoulder to find his brother – the instigator of the ridiculousness – crossing the office. 'Just one more meeting,' Theo murmured as he turned back to the windows, Ari joining him in several long strides to also stare at the view.

'I have news,' Ari said, eventually rousing himself from the hypnotic pull of the Athens skyline.

Theo side-eyed his brother. That sounded ominous. 'Oh?'

'Dimitri Kouris is back on the hook.'

'Really?'

Theo hadn't been convinced that keeping his face and other parts of his body out of the tabloids would have any effect on the stubborn old coot, but maybe Ari had been right.

It happened, occasionally.

'Yep.' Ari nodded. 'He's ready to sell.'

'That's...' Theo grinned at his brother. 'Incredible.' He pulled his brother in for a backslapping hug. Neither of them had wanted to let their grandfather down, and Ari had been beavering away determinedly to get things back on track for a couple of months now.

'Uh huh,' Ari agreed. 'There's just something he needs first.'

Oh, for the love of... Theo unhanded his brother. 'You're shitting me?' They were going to put more money in the man's pocket and save his damn company from going under. What else could he possibly need? 'A mariachi band? A kidney? A fucking unicorn?'

'He wants to spend some time with you.'

'Okay.' Theo's brow furrowed. That would be excruciating but he'd be willing to do it for the sake of the deal. 'Like, dinner? I could squeeze that in tonight.' It would delay him getting on the boat but it'd be worth it if it helped allay Dimitri's concerns about Theo's moral character. 'Or we can arrange something for when I get back from Crete?'

Ari shook his head. 'No. He wants to spend a couple of days with you.'

Theo blinked. 'What?'

'What can I say?' Ari shrugged. 'The man wants what he wants.'

Theo knew exactly what Dimitri wanted. He wanted to look Theo in the eye and get his measure. Because Dimitri Kouris, like Yannis Callisthenes, was an honourable man who believed that a man's word was his pledge.

But Theo didn't want to spend days pretending he was a changed man when he had every intention of getting back on the one-night-stand circuit when the four months was up.

An image of Tiffany flicked through his brain like a cloud skittering across the sky.

Yeah – she'd be his first call.

'Did you say yes?' he demanded.

Ari snorted. 'Of course I did.'

'Ari.' Theo almost choked. 'You know he's going to ask me to keep my pants zipped.' Something he probably wouldn't have said at a restaurant.

'And you're going to tell him you will.'

'No, I'm not.'

'Yes, you are.'

It was irritating how much his brother didn't give a rat's ass that he was the CEO of the company, and older. 'You want me to lie to him?'

Ari crossed his arms and let out a long-suffering sigh. 'I think if these past two months have taught you anything, it's that your life has been much less complicated without the tabloid drama, right?'

Theo had to admit not being followed around by paparazzi and reading utter *malakies* about himself online had been a very pleasant by-product of this dare.

'So,' Ari continued, 'if you're not out there flaunting a different woman each night on your arm at all the cool places, if you're just more discreet, for fuck's sake, I think Dimitri will call that a win.'

The cool places. It had been so long since he'd been out he'd forgotten all about them. He wasn't sure when the clubs of Athens or Milan or Barcelona had started losing their appeal, but all Theo could think about now was what was waiting for him on the *Nerida*.

Another image of Tiffany fluttered through his grey matter, and he stomped on it. The sea. Adventure. Crete. That was what was waiting for him, damn it.

'Fine,' Theo huffed. Being more discreet wouldn't kill him.

'But it's going to have to wait until I get back from Crete.' No way was he delaying that for anyone. Not for Dimitri Kouris or his grandfather.

'About that...' Ari said, trailing off as he turned back to the window.

Theo narrowed his eyes at his brother's profile. 'What about that?'

'He and his wife are going to be in town tomorrow on their way to Mykonos so I extended an invitation to them on your behalf to spend a couple of days with you on the *Nerida* doing some island-hopping, and you could drop them off there.'

Gaping was all Theo was capable of right now. This could not be happening.

'What?' Ari said, a smile tugging at his mouth as he glanced at Theo. 'It's on the way. Also, they're delighted.'

Theo couldn't believe what he was hearing. He'd been looking forward to this trip for the past two weeks so he could relax and get away from it all. Enjoy this amazing playground of islands and sea that were entwined into the fabric of his life and he got to call home.

And now he was going to have to entertain an old curmudgeon who'd wouldn't know a good time if it sat on his face.

'You know I'm your boss, right?'

Ari raised an eyebrow. 'You know I pay you, right?'

Neither was strictly true, but it was familiar patter for them. 'Fine,' Theo huffed. 'Two days.'

Ari grinned. 'Good. They'll be on board tomorrow afternoon at five to get settled in for dinner. Dimitri expressed a desire for calamari.'

Theo glared at his brother. Dimitri Kouris would get whatever the hell Maria put down in front of him.

Grinning, Ari slapped his brother on the back. 'Let me know

how it goes,' he said, backing away as Theo turned his glare on the view. 'Theo,' he called as he got to the door.

'Fine,' he snapped, not looking at his brother. 'He can have the damn calamari.'

'No, it's not...' Theo heard the seriousness in Ari's tone and half turned. 'I've done all I can but he's still a little hesitant. You need to be on your best behaviour. It's up to you to convince him now. For Pappou.'

Theo sighed at the not so subtle turning of the screw. 'Yeah, yeah. I'll play nice.'

Ari grinned. 'I kinda wish I was going to be there now.'

Theo brightened. 'Brilliant idea. Why don't you and Kelsey join us?' The more the merrier. Theo could demonstrate he was a huge proponent of family and, with more people to spread the conversational load, there'd be less opportunity for Dimitri to lecture.

'Ha. Good try. Even if she was back from London, the answer would still be no. You're on your own with this one.'

And with another grin, he swaggered out the door.

* * *

After a night of brooding about the poisoned chalice Ari had handed him, Theo had woken with a plan so brilliant for the next two days he'd even impressed himself. Dimitri Kouris might be here willingly and be open again to signing on the dotted line but, as Ari had suggested, he wasn't convinced that Theo had turned his ways around.

So what better way to seal the deal than showing the man he was reformed than by producing a fiancée?

Would that be lying to him? Yes. Was that particularly honourable? No. But sometimes a little bending of the truth didn't hurt. Especially if it meant they could save the old fool's company and fulfil a promise to their grandfather. And it also meant he could avoid Dimitri's inevitable demand, which would have led Theo to tell an outright lie direct to the older man's face.

Having a fiancée on the boat would imply that Theo's playboy days were done, and Dimitri wouldn't even need to ask Theo to keep it zipped.

Win-win.

All he had to do now was persuade Tiffany to partner with him in the pretence. He'd flipped through a dozen alternatives in his brain but kept coming back to her. For starters, the other options, although living in Athens, were all on his one-and-done list, and the last thing he wanted was for any of them to think they had another shot.

Because nobody got another shot.

And sure, they all knew that, but could he blame them if they read a little too much into him calling again after he'd very firmly told them he wouldn't? Even if he went to great pains to lay out the boundaries of this little venture?

Then he'd have an even bigger problem on his hands. Possibly more if the woman in question decided to put her irritation into something that could harm his reputation, like an article for a tabloid magazine.

Theo could see the headlines now. *Theo Callisthenes's Two-Day Fiancée.*

Women giving stories about him to the press hadn't been without precedence, which had never particularly bothered Theo. They'd had their fifteen seconds of fame and earned themselves some money in the process. But even if Dimitri had signed on the line by the time an article appeared, he wouldn't want to make a fool of the man.

He could, of course, formalise the agreement with someone, very specifically outlining roles and expectations, but he only had eight hours before Dimitri and Helena stepped foot on the *Nerida*, and he didn't want that kind of paper trail anyway.

Also, if he was going to do this, it couldn't be with someone he didn't know very well or who didn't really know him outside of the bedroom. They were going to need to be convincing.

Dimitri might not have been up to the challenge, as he'd aged, of steering his company through the multitude of complex economic challenges that had dominated the last decade, but he was no dummy. He'd be able to sniff out a fake very quickly and there'd be no deal after that.

Which led him back to Tiffany.

Of all the people on this boat, she knew him best, a fact he did not stop to ponder or question because what exactly did that say about his life? Sure, she didn't know him like his *mamaka* or his *yiayia*, but Theo let precious few women close, which meant she knew him better than the vast majority.

He'd never told any of the women he took to bed about his childhood or his love affair with the sea. He hadn't eaten with them around a table more than once and not without it being a prelude to something else. They hadn't seen him with his parents or his brother or extended family. They hadn't stood around a blackjack table for seven nights in a row listening to some of his closest friends spill some of his most embarrassing stories.

But Tiffany had. Which meant she was perfect for the role.

It was that simple. And that complicated. Because the other thing they had going was chemistry. He knew it. She knew it. His friends knew it. Hell, he was pretty sure the crew knew it. And even though he'd been trying to ignore it, it never really went away.

It was always just there.

Every time he glanced up from something and she was in his line of vision. Every time they passed each other on the boat. Every time their fingers brushed when she handed him a salt-shaker or their eyes met when he was giving crew instructions, or she laughed at something he said.

Simmering. Seething. Smouldering. Just waiting for one of them to blink.

Chemistry, of course, was great for what he was proposing. But on a boat that sometimes didn't feel anywhere near big enough for the two of them, it felt a little like he was playing with fire.

Then there was the biggest problem of all. Tiffany. He had to convince Tiffany that this wasn't some sleazy ploy to get her into his master suite. That it was a favour he was asking, and that he wouldn't take advantage of the situation – because that would be dishonourable – despite the fact she would, of course, have to sleep in his master suite.

If he failed to convince her then he'd have to go it alone the next two days with Dimitri and Helena and try to avoid any promises he wasn't prepared to keep. But he wasn't above offering Tiffany some juicy incentives. Because now he'd convinced himself this was the best course of action, he really, really didn't want to have to face Dimitri without her.

Without his fiancée.

'No. Absolutely not. Are you nuts?' Tiffany glared at Theo, not quite believing that he could so calmly lay out this unhinged plan. 'What on earth makes you think I would agree to something like this? Something so... illogical and... ludicrous and... harebrained?'

Not giving him time to answer any of her rapid-fire incredulous questions, she started to pace. Had he chosen the wheelhouse deliberately so the rest of the crew wouldn't hear her wailing at him?

'Do you think this is the goddamn Middle Ages?' she demanded. 'Where men used women as bargaining chips? Did you have a stroke? Should I call the paramedics? Oh my God—'

She stopped pacing abruptly and felt for the pulse in her neck.

'Have I had a stroke? And this is some white-light-hovering-above-the-earth-while-my-life-hangs-in-the-balance kind of thing? Do you have aspirin? I think you're supposed to take aspirin if you're having a stroke.'

Okay, maybe she wasn't having a stroke, but she was definitely winding herself up into a panic attack. Her heart was racing and it was hard to catch her breath, unlike him who was watching her calmly like he was patiently waiting for her to run out of steam, which really lit her fuse.

Not to mention he looked... hot and calm in his goddamn shorts and T-shirt that outlined every muscle in his chest, quads and ass. His hair was the only thing not perfectly put together, looking somewhat dishevelled, like he'd finger-combed it into submission.

But hot dishevelled, standing there with his hand resting casually on the wheel all Orlando Bloom again. While she was over here having a panic attack.

'You should breathe now,' he suggested mildly.

And her fuse went kaboom.

'Do not,' she hissed, taking up the pacing once more, 'tell me to breathe.'

If Tiffany had found it hard to believe Theo had never been in a relationship before, she didn't any longer. No man who'd spent more than one night with the female of the species would tell any woman, in the middle of an argument/yelling jag, to take a breath.

Sure, she was starting to feel a little lightheaded, but rookie move, dude.

Wisely, Theo held up his hands in a surrender motion and let her pace it out of her system. When she was done, she pulled up in front of him, folded her arms and reiterated her initial response. 'No. Absolutely not.'

'Okay, that is of course your prerogative, but—'

And she was off again with the pacing, gesticulating with her hands to emphasise her points. 'You're asking me to lie to a person I don't even know. And his wife. And act as some moony, lovesick girl while playing hostess.'

'Moony and/or lovesick not required.'

Ignoring him, Tiffany whipped around. 'I suppose I'm to grace your bed, too?'

He shrugged. 'It would be tough to explain if you didn't accompany me to my suite.'

Well, gosh darn it, she'd hate to put him in a tough spot.

Tiffany folded her arms again. Mostly because she was cranky, a little to hide the sudden interest of her nipples in them sleeping together. 'Didn't you just stand there and tell me in justifying this ridiculous proposal that Dimitri Kouris is an old-fashioned man? It sounds like he'd probably admire your restraint.'

'I'm sure he would but... there's no way he'd believe it. Unfortunately, my reputation precedes me and you sleeping elsewhere would make him suspicious as to the validity of our relationship, and this needs to be convincing.'

'How convenient,' she said with an acid-sweet smile.

'It's a big suite,' he said with a twist of his lips, 'and I have every intention of winning the dare with Ari. I'll sleep on the couch.'

Tiffany had been in Theo's suite often. She cleaned it most mornings and slotted freshly laundered clothes into his cupboard on the regular. And it was big. But the couch was made for lounging, not sleeping.

Good. She hoped it wrecked his back.

'Why a fiancée?' she demanded as more and more of her brain recovered from the shock and was able to process things more clearly. 'Why not a girlfriend?' She was, after all, a girl who he'd been very friendly with – for approximately sixteen hours.

She could pull that off.

'A girlfriend wouldn't be enough for him. A girlfriend says, *this one for now*. A fiancée says, *I chose you forever*. There's no commitment in a girlfriend.'

This one for now? Bloody hell, the man really had no clue about the nature of long-term relationships. 'You really think that?' Tiffany might have only been in a couple of semi-serious situationships before, which made her no expert, but she knew plenty of people committed themselves to one person without a ring.

'He thinks that.' Theo huffed out a breath. 'Look...'

His brow pulled down as he shoved his hands in his pockets and, no matter how tempted she was, Tiffany did not check out how the action tightened the fabric of those shorts across the bulge behind his zipper.

'I get it, you have your objections and you're allowed.'

'Why thank you,' she muttered sarcastically.

'But can we just cut to the chase here? As I've already said, Ari and I are just trying to save the man's company from ruin, even if he does act like he's holding all the damn cards. This deal was on the hook and my last appearance in the tabloids ruined it. So I'm trying to fix it and I can't think of a more definitive way of demonstrating I'm a reformed man than by producing a fiancée.'

Tiffany supposed there was some warped kind of sense to it on paper, but that didn't explain why Dimitri Kouris gave a rat's ass about Theo's well-publicised sex life.

'I don't get it? Why does he care about you being reformed?'

Watching the sudden guardedness of Theo's expression put an itch up Tiffany's spine. These two men definitely had history. And, for a moment, as the angle of his jaw blanched white, she thought Theo wasn't going to answer. Then he sighed and turned around to face the windows, giving her his back as he looked out over the bow of the boat.

'There was this girl. Back in the day.'

Uh oh. That didn't sound good. 'Okay.'

'Angelika Konstantinides.'

'Okay.'

Her anger tempering a little, Tiffany crossed to stand beside him but kept some distance. He obviously didn't talk about whatever had happened very much, and she wanted to see his eyes as he did. Turning around, she leaned her ass against the console, making it easier to see Theo's face without getting a crick in her neck.

Glancing at her briefly, he returned his gaze to the windows. 'Growing up, our families were close,' he began. 'We lived in the same neighbourhood, we socialised with them, we went on ski holidays and joint family road trips with them. We even all went to Australia once, when we were eleven. For New Year's Eve on Sydney Harbour.'

Tiffany suppressed the urge to roll her eyes at the utter decadence of that. It wasn't Theo's fault he'd been born into the lap of luxury.

'Our fathers did business occasionally.'

'He's in shipping as well?'

'No.' Theo shook his head. 'The family owns the Eros hotel chain.'

'Ah.' Tiffany blinked at the name drop. Very posh.

'Angelika and I are the same age. We went to the same schools, we hung out with the same people, went to the same parties. We were good friends. The first time I ever got drunk on ouzo was with Angelika.'

A smile softened the serious lines of his face. It was clearly a fond memory, and Tiffany was shocked by a sudden visceral surge of jealousy rising like hot bile.

What the hell?

Jealousy? She had no claim on Theo and even if she had, this girl was from his past. His distant past.

'She was great. She *is* great,' he corrected, frowning at his slip. 'Our parents always used to joke that we'd end up married and we laughed about it together because they weren't that subtle at times. We'd roll our eyes at their matchmaking and ponder how old we'd be before they gave up on the whole idea. Sometimes, when we knew they were watching, we'd hold hands and whisper to each other just to yank their chains because it was so ridiculous.'

Tiffany had a bad feeling she knew where this was going. 'Was it though?'

'Yes.' For the first time since he'd started talking about it, he met her gaze. 'It was Angelika. She was like my sister. We even used each other for cover. Going out together somewhere because we knew our parents would let us, but splitting up to be with friends or even dates with other people we knew our parents wouldn't approve of. And then...'

Theo's gaze shifted back to the glass, the bright sunshine highlighting the sudden storm clouds dimming the blue of his eyes. Tiffany waited for him to continue.

'We went out to this club with a bunch of friends. We'd both just finished school and it was the end of a great summer which we'd pretty much spent together. I was going off to London. She was going to the US. There was drinking and dancing and she and her friends were chatting to some guys, and there was this woman who kept giving me the eye across the room. She was probably twenty years older than me but she didn't seem to mind, and when she slid up and asked me if I wanted to have some fun, I sure as hell didn't mind.'

'But...' Tiffany quirked an eyebrow. 'Angelika minded?'

'I don't know, it never occurred to me to check.' The exasperation in his voice backed up his statement. 'I just took her hand and we slipped out into the alley at the back and we' – he side-eyed her briefly – 'did our thing.'

'And Angelika followed?'

'God, no.' He grimaced. 'But there were some paps at the club because it was popular with celebrities and they'd photographed Angelika and me going in holding hands, and when this woman and I became aware of our surroundings again, there were two paps at the end of the alley with cameras, snapping away.'

Tiffany gaped. 'What? That's terrible.'

Theo shrugged. 'Welcome to my life.' Sucking in a breath, he continued the saga. 'So I took off after them, running around the front of the club, and managed to snag one of them and punch him in the face, which was... witnessed by a cop and I got arrested.'

'Oh Jesus.' She hadn't expected that development.

He chuckled at her startled reply, which seemed to relax him, the hands jammed in his pockets now sliding loosely onto the wheel. 'Only briefly,' he assured. 'But, yeah, it was a hell of a night. My parents were furious.'

'I'm assuming hers were as well.'

'Not as furious as they were when pictures of me and their daughter arriving at a club and me in the back alley of that club two hours later having sex with an older woman were plastered side by side over every Greek news site in existence.'

'Oof.' Tiffany winced.

'But the worst part was how distraught Angelika was about it all. It was awful.' He grimaced as if the memory of that moment was still seared on his brain. 'She turned up at the door with one of the tabloids in her hands, yelling and bawling her eyes out. She accused me of making a fool of her and disrespecting her, which was fair enough. The pictures of us entering the club did make it look like we were together and that I was cheating on her right under her nose. She also said that I'd betrayed her and our families' wishes about us marrying and... how could I because she was in love with me and... I was a callous, unfeeling bastard.'

Tiffany winced some more. She could only imagine how that must have gone down.

'I swear to you,' he said, meeting her gaze, his blue eyes piercing her as if looking for her understanding, 'I had no idea she felt that way.'

For what it was worth, Tiffany believed him. Sincerity oozed from his eyes and tinged his voice along with a faint note of disbelief. Like he still struggled with what had happened.

'I thought she'd thought this whole running joke between our families was just that. But apparently, she'd been secretly in love with me for years and because I never told her straight out that I didn't love her and that I didn't want to marry her, she'd thought I'd come around, and she'd been waiting for me to make the first move.'

Yeesh. Poor Theo. Even if he had missed the signs, which he may well have – teenage boys weren't known for their emotional intelligence – it was obvious he'd been blindsided and felt dreadful.

'If I'd known how she felt I would have had conversations with her earlier. I would never have let it get to that point. She was one of my oldest, dearest friends and to see her hurt her like that and know I was responsible?' He shuddered. 'That was really awful.'

It hit Tiffany then, the realisation dawning suddenly. 'That's why you're a strict one-and-done guy.' It made perfect sense now.

'Yup.' He nodded. 'I made up my mind after that terrible confrontation that I would never again be unclear with a woman. And so that none of them would ever be in any doubt, I decided I'd never offer anything more than a one-night thing.'

For a moment, Tiffany wondered how different Theo's life might be without that early negative experience. If he'd been allowed to do stupid things like most people growing into adulthood, screwing up without it being splashed all over the papers and becoming monumentally consequential for him and Angelika and their families.

Would he be wifed up by now like all the other male role models in his family? Have his own kids running around? A funny little pang pinged Tiffany's chest. She actually felt a little sorry for the guy.

'What happened then?'

'She went into a bit of a depression for a while, delayed going to the US. Everyone, including me, was really worried. And it caused a huge rift between the families for a few years.'

'But not any more?'

'No. Angelika slowly came out of her funk with some help and things got back on an even keel for her and for us. We started to talk about how it all evolved and she was really sorry about not being honest with me about her feelings, and I apologised for my complete cluelessness.' He gave a harsh half laugh. 'And we became friends again, which also healed the split between our parents. She went to the US and kicked hotel ass and met a guy who she married, and they have three children and she's very happy.'

'All's well that ends well, huh?'

'Right.' He shot her a rueful smile.

'So...' Tiffany frowned, still obviously missing a piece. 'How does Dimitri fit into all of this? Or does he take it upon himself to hold grudges on behalf of women generally?'

Theo gave her a thin smile. 'Dimitri is Angelika's godfather. And with no children of their own, he absolutely dotes on her. And even though everyone else, including her actual father, who I was pretty sure was going to kill me when those photos came out, has moved on, Dimitri has not. Good friends with my grandfather or not, he's not willing to let bygones be bygones.'

Okay. Tiffany got it now. Sort of. Even if it did sound like she was caught in the middle of a Greek tragedy. Still didn't mean she was on board with what Theo was proposing. 'Thank you for that info, it all makes a little more sense now. But...' She shook her head. 'I don't think us pretending to be engaged is the way to go with Dimitri. It seems like he values honesty, and you're suggesting a deception.'

'It's not ideal and I'm not okay with deceiving him,' Theo admitted. 'But trust me, I know old Greek men, and this one in particular, and I'm trying to give him a way to save face as well. He's proud and the one person offering him a lifeline to stop his company from going under is the one he denounced as being an untrustworthy playboy at every opportunity all those years ago. But if I'm a better man, he gets to be gracious and forgive and be the bigger person and magnanimously accept what is essentially a hand out.'

Tiffany blinked. Gah. She had not expected the man to be so persuasive over this preposterous idea. But hell if he wasn't winning her over. As if sensing her wavering, Theo pressed his advantage. 'Please, it's only two days.'

'And three nights.' Of utter temptation.

Because, apart from the deception, that was what was occupying her brain the most right now. Couch or not, a no-sex dare or not, being in the same room as him and a luxurious king-sized bed may not be the smartest move. The other bed they'd spent the night in had been pretty freaking fancy too but, rolling around in a hotel bed for a night then walking away was very different to spending several nights in a man's bedroom under the pretence of an intimate relationship and being privy to the most personal things about him.

His brand of toothpaste/cologne/soap. His brand of under-wear. Did he do that thing where he shaved in front of the mirror with a towel wrapped around his waist? Did he use an electric razor or did he wet shave using foam and a razor? Did he dress in the ensuite or did he walk buck naked from the bath-room to the bedroom?

How was she supposed to go back below deck after that and act like they were still boss and employee for another month? A line she'd already found hard enough to walk these last weeks.

And what in the hell would the rest of the crew think?

'What if I were to' – he turned on his side so his hip was leaning against the wheel and crossed his arms, a speculative gleam in his eyes – 'sweeten the pot?'

14

Tiffany raised an eyebrow as the speculation morphed into calculation. It was chillingly rapid. The businessman had emerged and he seemed much more in his comfort zone now. Relaxed even, like he knew there was a deal to be made.

Asking her, presenting reasoned arguments, throwing himself on her mercy, had put the ball in her court. Had given her too much power and not produced the desired result.

She imagined he usually operated from a position of strength, and needing her like this had put him on the back foot.

But he was in his natural habitat. Incentivising was his territory.

What shape would his bribe take? Did he think she'd agree to this plan if he was to buy her a diamond ring or a sapphire necklace or a shiny red Porsche? What exactly did this hotshot business guy think her weakness was? Because Tiffany cared for none of those things.

The plain fact of the matter was helping a proud old man save face was probably impetus enough for her to agree to being a billionaire's fake fiancée.

He just didn't know her that well.

'What if I was to buy your brother a new place that's bigger and better than the one he has at the moment. A place he can live and create and display his art so he can just get on with being an artist without worrying about a mortgage or rent or the whims of a landlord.'

Tiffany blinked as the stunning offer dropped like a boulder into a deep black lake between them, plunging down, down, down but never finding the bottom, taking her stomach with it for the ride.

Well, hell. Maybe he did know her. Because he sure as hell managed to find her Achilles heel.

And her first instinct was to jump on it and grab it with both hands, but Tiffany had learned from the divorce between her parents that being beholden to someone financially could end up disastrously if that relationship ever broke down and the other party held the financial purse strings to your life. Her father – despite being caught with his pants down – had screwed over the mother of his children for every cent he could.

Mikey had also learned that lesson when he'd left Balmain Downs with zero financial support from their father.

'And leave it up to the whims of a billionaire instead? When my brother's livelihood becomes part of your property portfolio? An asset that the company can decide, at any moment, to divest themselves of?'

Theo's eyes turned to two chips of ice. 'It would be his, free and clear.' His voice went as chilly as his eyes; he clearly was not impressed that she had called his integrity into question. 'A gift. No takebacks.'

Yeah... until there was.

All she did was cock an eyebrow. That was it. But he was

getting good at reading her eyebrows. His mouth thinned in displeasure, but he didn't give up either.

'Okay... what about this. I know a lot of people throughout Europe in the art world. I could pick up my phone and have his art displayed in any number of galleries known for promoting emerging artists. A friend of my mother's books exhibitions that do the avant-garde circuit from Porto to Prague. I can also arrange very quickly to have several pieces of his on every Ōceanós cruise ship in the fleet.'

Okay... this proposal was a much different prospect. This wouldn't be about Mikey relying on someone else to take care of his financial burden. This would be giving her brother an opportunity to prove himself in the art world and give him the financial means to not rely on anyone else. Not Theo. Not her, even. It would be opening a door that hadn't been open to him before, but it would be up to Mikey to make the most of it. Take the openings that came from it, the connections, to grow and prosper. He would be in control of his destiny, not reliant on the largess of a third party.

Bubbles of excitement frothed in Tiffany's blood like a shaken bottle of champagne as a hope took flight in her chest. It was perfect.

Damn Theo Callisthenes to hell.

Breathing in slowly, she looked him in the eye. 'And you really think we can pull this off? That Dimitri will actually believe it?'

Theo smiled. He knew capitulation when he saw it. To his credit, he didn't gloat, he just got on with business. 'Oh, he'll believe it.'

'Why? Because you're that convincing?' Which was an idiot question. He'd convinced her to go through with it, hadn't he?

'No.' Another smile tugged at his beautiful mouth. '*We're* that convincing. Because we have chemistry. Every time I look at you I want to touch you. I want to drag you close and kiss you until neither of us can breathe.'

His voice had turned to gravel, so low and rough it was almost a physical caress, and his fingers curled around the steering wheel, his knuckles whitening like he was in imminent danger of following through and he was barely keeping himself in check.

A pulse beat slow and thick through her ears and between her legs.

'I want to drag you to my suite, lay you on my bed, strip you naked, push your legs as wide apart as they'll go and feast on your pussy until you beg me to stop because I haven't been able to get the taste of you off my tongue or out of my brain for months.'

Tiffany's clit contracted so hard at that visual it caused her breath to hitch, which was loud in the silence of the wheelhouse. Theo had put her right back in the middle of the night he'd proved to her just how well a Greek billionaire could give head. And he'd made her slick and achy in the process.

'And I know you feel this crazy chemistry, too.'

Tiffany swallowed hard. Because she did. Every time she looked at him, she was reminded how good it had felt to have him inside her, big and thick, rammed to the hilt, puffing filthy Greek words into her neck.

Her expression must have told him all he needed to know because he just nodded and said, 'That's what Dimitri and his wife will see. They won't need any convincing.'

Swallowing, Tiffany nodded. With her throat suddenly dry as the Sahara, she didn't trust her voice for a beat or two. 'And what do we tell them?' she continued huskily. 'About us? They'll have questions.'

'Keep things as close to the truth as possible. We met at the wedding. You're Kelsey's best friend and have worked on several Ōceanós boats for the last eight years. You've been a guest on the yacht but things have turned serious and I just popped the question last night.'

She looked at him doubtfully. 'What if we contradict each other?'

'It'll be fine,' he assured. 'Just follow my lead.'

Tiffany wished she could be as confident as Theo. But she wasn't. She was going to have to be though, because Theo was offering Mikey his first big break and she had no doubt that her brother would meet the challenge and exceed it; she just had to play her part.

And if that meant she had to smile and laugh and make goo-goo eyes at Theo, then that was what she'd do.

'Here.' He reached into his back pocket, pulled out a slim wallet and handed over a black AMEX card. 'Go out and buy yourself some suitable clothes for the next few days.'

Tiffany's hand trembled as she took it, not quite believing how fast this was all happening or the fact she was about to live out some *Pretty Woman* fantasy. She opened her mouth to object but shut it again. She supposed Theo would want her to look the part, and it wouldn't be any hardship to go and buy a bunch of beautiful things on Theo's dime all in the name of helping her brother.

'They arrive at five,' he said as her fingers closed around the slim plastic card.

Tiffany nodded absently, a part of her still trying to comprehend the surreal turn of events.

One thing was for sure – she wouldn't be telling Kelsey about this one...

* * *

Any concerns Theo had that Tiffany would be able to pull this off were immediately allayed as she stepped out onto the main deck two minutes after Dimitri and Helena Kouris came on board.

She'd been away until after two, returning to the ship with several bags from exclusive boutiques. He'd told her that the crew had been informed of the situation and her bag was in his suite, and she could get ready in there. And then he'd presented her with an oval, two-carat opal and diamond ring and she'd visibly paled.

He'd thought she'd appreciate the Australian touch, but it wasn't until he'd assured her it was a loaner that she actually put it on her finger.

But here she was greeting his guests with all the aplomb and graciousness of royalty in a silky kaftan-style dress. It had a deep V at the cleavage and whorls of blue as fascinating as the Aegean as the fabric flowed against her body like water.

Dimitri, in long trousers and a white button-down shirt featuring panels of traditional Greek geometric embroidery, looked to Theo for context. His steely grey hair was perfectly coifed as he switched effortlessly from Greek to English, his accent heavier than Theo's.

'To what do we owe the pleasure?'

He may have been charmed by Tiffany's bright smile, the quick offering of her hand and her own introduction, but the eyes he turned on Theo showed his displeasure. Dimitri was clearly miffed at having to share Theo and having his attention divided.

'I asked Tiffany to marry me last night,' he said, sliding an arm around her waist. He felt a small flinch before she relaxed and he snugged her close. 'To my eternal relief' – huge fucking relief – 'she said yes.'

To say Dimitri was blindsided was an understatement. He looked like a landed fish, mouth open, gawping at the two of them. Helena, looking elegant as ever in a linen pantsuit, recovered first. 'Theo Callisthenes, you kept this one quiet,' she murmured with teasing accusation as she hugged him, her multitude of thin bangles tinkling at his back.

'It's been a whirlwind,' he said.

She turned to Tiffany and gave her a quick fierce hug. 'Congratulations, my dear. You have your hands full with this one.'

'Oh, I think Theo knows which side his bread is buttered on,' Tiffany joked.

Helena laughed. 'It looks like *you* have your hands full, Theo.'

Theo grinned at Helena. 'I love a woman who can keep me on my toes.'

'There haven't been too many of them,' she said.

Theo shook his head. 'There have not.' None, in fact. Women had fallen over themselves to fit in with him, not the other way around.

Dimitri, who still hadn't spoken, finally found his voice, even if it was little more than a splutter. 'But how?' he demanded. 'Ari never said anything about this.'

'That's because,' Theo supplied, 'apart from the crew, you and Helena are the first ones to know.'

Dimitri perked up. He clearly liked the idea of being in the loop with this exclusive piece of news. Underneath it all, like those old Greek fishermen mending their nets, he was an inveterate gossip. Still, he wasn't completely sold. 'Ari never even mentioned you were seeing anyone.'

Theo shrugged. 'You ever meet someone so special you were

afraid that if you talked about it or told anyone you might jinx it?'

Dimitri looked at his wife and reached for her hand. 'Yes.'

There was a beat where the older couple, both in their eighties, just smiled at each other, and Theo could see the entire history of their relationship in that interaction. The good times, the bad times, the moment their eyes had first met and they'd fallen in love. And as much as Dimitri had been a thorn in Theo's side for almost two decades, a blinding white-hot spike of jealousy lanced his chest.

He was jealous of what this old pain-in-the-ass had in his life. Theo could buy and sell him a hundred times over and his beloved company was on the skids, yet Dimitri had something Theo did not. Something money couldn't buy. He had a woman by his side that even after fifty years of marriage and encroaching financial disaster still looked at him like he was the centre of her world.

And vice versa.

It was the oddest thing because Theo had been actively avoiding just that and yet, looking at them, he realised that perhaps he'd been missing out.

'Well, I guess that's how it's been with us.' He glanced down into Tiffany's face the same time she looked up at him and smiled, and hell if his heart didn't give a mule-sized kick inside his chest. Returning his attention to Dimitri, he said, 'It's been quick and it's surprised us, but after a long time – for both of us – not wanting anything serious, we knew this was different.'

He'd told Tiffany to keep their lies as close to the truth as possible, and it was surprising for Theo to realise that was exactly what he was doing. Tiffany was different. Unlike any woman he'd ever spent time with.

'I did notice,' Dimitri said, beaming at them both as if he'd somehow orchestrated it himself, 'that you've not been seen in any tabloids of late. I thought it was to appease me.'

Theo smiled. No flies on Dimitri. 'No, sir,' he lied. 'It's because I'm smitten with this one.' The second statement, however, didn't feel like a lie, and Theo steeled himself to look into her face again and not let the way she smiled back whammy him another time.

'Aww,' she murmured, her hand covering her chest as she gave a dramatic sigh, a smile twitching her mouth and sparkling in her eyes before she looked at the old Greek couple who were revelling in the PDA. 'Isn't he the sweetest?'

Dimitri chuckled. 'Women...' he said with a conspiratorial wink at Theo. 'They like to emasculate us, no?'

Helena made a *pfft* noise as she flapped her husband's teasing comment aside. 'Enough of that. Show us that gorgeous ring you're wearing.'

Dutifully, Tiffany held out her hand for the inspection, the opal flashing fire and the diamonds sparkling. Theo was pleased he'd decided to go for big and flashy. Helena Kouris, and by default her husband, appreciated a show of love in the medium of jewellery as evidenced by the rock on her finger.

'The opal is gorgeous,' she said, inspecting it closely. 'And are they diamonds?'

Tiffany nodded. 'From the Kimberley region, which is not far from where I grew up. And the opal is from Coober Pedy, which is practically built on opal mining. It was so thoughtful of Theo to give me a ring that reminded me of home.'

Theo hadn't thought she'd listened to any stats about the ring when he'd given it to her, but clearly, she had, which both surprised and delighted him, as had the personalisation of the story for her guests, who'd eaten it up.

'See,' Tiffany said, humour lacing her voice as she addressed Dimitri, 'sweet.'

He grinned good-naturedly as he rolled his eyes and Helena laughed. 'Australia.' Dimitri breathed the word in a hushed kind of reverence. 'We've never been but we've always wanted to. I'd love to know more about where you're from. Your family. Your earlier life. And all about the snakes.'

Tiffany laughed as Helena put her hand on her husband's arm. 'Dimitri,' she scolded lightly, 'don't overwhelm the poor girl. At least wait until we're eating.'

And that was Theo's cue. 'Yes. Dinner will be served at seven out here on the deck. In the meantime, Kelly' – he gestured behind them to Kelly, who had been hovering in the background – 'will show you around the boat and to your suite. I'm going up to get us underway. We'll anchor off Hydra tonight. Feel free to come out onto the deck and enjoy the afternoon as we sail.'

Kelly smiled at the couple as she shook their hands and said, 'This way, please.'

Theo and Tiffany, still arm in arm, watched them as they followed and he almost sagged in relief when they were finally out of sight. 'Thank you,' he murmured as he slowly eased his arm from around her.

But she didn't step away like he'd suspected she might; she just looked at him as she exhaled an exaggerated breath. 'So far so good.'

He grinned. 'We can do this.'

'Yes but' – she bugged her hazel eyes at him – 'we'll probably go to hell for it.'

Theo chuckled. That might have been a worry for someone more religious, but it didn't hold a lot of sway with him. 'Wouldn't you rather laugh with the sinners than cry with the saints?'

Cocking an eyebrow, she said, 'I let you utterly debauch me after knowing you for two hours, what do you think?'

Her statement was like a cattle prod to Theo's cock as he remembered all too well how thoroughly she had also debauched him. She sure had a way with that mouth of hers – for talking and other things.

Grinning, he said, 'See you in an hour or so.'

15

Theo joined them aft mid-deck almost two hours later. He'd just dropped anchor off Hydra a distance from the other boats bobbing in the Aegean closer to the island. Dimitri and Helena may want to go to the island in the morning, in which case Simon could tender them all to shore, but for now it was easier to not have to manoeuvre the huge superyacht into a crowded harbour for just one night.

The sound of voices greeted him as he stepped out, and Theo smiled to himself as Tiffany chatted away with Dimitri and Helena like she'd known them all her life. She was a natural at this fake fiancée charm offensive. He'd half expected Dimitri would join him on the bridge, but Tiffany had clearly charmed and waylaid him, and damn if that didn't make him want to kiss her senseless.

But thinking about kissing her was really not helpful.

Kelly handed him a beer as he claimed the spot next to Tiffany on the lounge.

'Theo,' Helena exclaimed. 'This is breathtaking.'

But he only had eyes for Tiffany, her cheeks flushed from a

combination of champagne and the warmth of the late afternoon sunshine, strands of her loose hair being picked up by the light breeze. She seemed happy and relaxed – in her element, even – which grabbed at his gut.

Also, the urge to debauch her on this couch grabbed at his balls. And squeezed.

'I know,' he replied as he slid his hand onto Tiffany's thigh. She didn't startle this time, just smiled at him before returning her attention to their guests.

Helena laughed. 'I meant the scenery.'

Still staring at Tiffany, Theo muttered, 'So did I.'

Dragging his eyes off Tiffany, he glanced up in time to catch the couple exchanging a look. They were clearly buying the show and Theo didn't even feel guilty because he wasn't lying about how he was feeling right now.

He was enjoying Tiffany's company and the addictive sizzle of chemistry this fake relationship had permitted to flourish. It zapped through every cell in his body until he buzzed with awareness of her.

'Dinner is served,' Kelly announced as she approached. 'We have the most succulent, melt-in-your-mouth calamari tonight. Chef has truly outdone herself.'

Dimitri nodded approvingly at Theo, beaming as he stood and offered one arm to his wife, the other to Tiffany – greedy bastard – who took it graciously with a small wink in his direction and, irrationally, Theo's fingers itched to snatch her away.

So he shoved them in his pocket and followed them to the beautifully laid table.

And Kelly was right, Maria had outdone herself with the calamari and the other three dishes they were served as the water shimmered with the colours of the sunset. Gold, pink, purple then silver as the sun slipped from sight and the lights of Hydra popped from the shore.

Conversation was lively and he didn't have to worry about any contradictions as Tiffany mostly spoke about her life growing up on a massive cattle station in Australia. Dimitri and Helena listened, clearly rapt by the tales she wove. She was utterly charming and by the end of the night they were both enamoured.

He knew how they felt.

The chat did eventually swing around to their relationship, but the questions weren't difficult. Just how they met, which morphed into Tiffany's friendship with Kelsey and then how amazing she'd been for Ari. And then the baby, of course. Which led to the most sticky question – for Theo anyway.

'And will you two be having your own babies soon?' Dimitri asked.

It was a common enough question for newly engaged couples, so it wasn't exactly out of leftfield. Theo just hadn't had it on his horizon because kids had never been part of his picture.

Tiffany didn't skip a beat though. 'Of course. Eventually.' She smiled at Theo who returned it, but it felt wooden and fake compared to the easy tilt of her mouth. 'He wants six kids.' Turning back to Dimitri, she laughed. 'We compromised on three. Two boys and a girl according to him and his crystal ball.'

Theo's gut clenched at the visceral slug of the images suddenly invading his head. Tiffany's belly swollen with his child. Being at her side as their baby entered the world. Two little blue-eyed, brown-haired boys and a little girl with chocolate curls and eyes just like her *mamaka*, all running to him with their arms open when he got home from work.

It was the antithesis of what he'd wanted from life but now, he wasn't so sure and the whole world seemed to suddenly tilt on an axis. What was wrong with him?

He'd had a vasectomy, for fuck's sake.

She smiled again as she leaned in towards Dimitri a little and lowered her voice conspiratorially. 'I think he also has the names picked out but he's denying it because he doesn't want to spook me.'

Dimitri chuckled but it soon faded. 'We couldn't have children,' he said wistfully.

Helena slid her hand into her husband's. 'It broke my heart,' she admitted.

'Oh. I'm so sorry to hear that,' Tiffany murmured, her voice tinged with empathy.

Smiling graciously, Helena shrugged. 'It was God's will and we've been lucky in other ways.'

But the ache and resignation in Helena's voice told its own story, making Theo look at the couple anew. For the first time since Dimitri had declared his intention to make Theo rue the day he'd embarrassed Angelika, he actually felt sorry for the older man. Pots and pots of money – back in the day – and he hadn't been able to give the person he loved the most in the world the one thing she wanted the most.

How gutting would something like that be to Theo's ego? How impotent would it make him feel? No wonder Dimitri had been so outraged at Theo's treatment of Angelika.

'Still.' Dimitri cleared his throat. 'We were blessed with a goddaughter and she has been the light of our life.'

Even if Angelika had just been on his mind, Theo hadn't expected Dimitri to mention her in front of Tiffany. He may be cantankerous but he was always polite. Looking across at the old man now, Theo didn't think it had been deliberate, but he really wished he hadn't as an awkward pall descended between them.

'Oh, yes, Theo told me.' Tiffany nodded matter-of-factly, either oblivious to, or completely ignoring, the pall, and Theo held his breath, trying to project with his eyes that she should abandon the topic, but she kept forging onwards. 'Angelika, right?'

Dimitri's brow furrowed, emphasising the wrinkles of his forehead. 'Theo told you about Angelika?'

'Of course.' She shrugged a shoulder. 'We don't have any secrets.'

He turned an appraising gaze on Theo, who met and held it unflinchingly. It had been seventeen years, it was long resolved, and it was time the old man let it go.

'I admire that he told me actually,' Tiffany continued, sliding her hand on top of his, mimicking the older couple. 'It was an incident in his life from a long time ago that he sincerely regrets and still feels it as a stain on his character, which I think speaks volumes about the kind of man he is. The kind that admits when he made a mistake and accepts responsibility for it.'

Still looking at Theo, Dimitri nodded slowly. 'There is certainly honour in that,' he agreed before his gaze shifted back to Tiffany. 'Theo is lucky to have you.'

'I know, right?' She grinned impishly, and Dimitri and Helena laughed as the undercurrent of tension snapped in two. 'I tell him that all the time.'

'And does he believe you?' Helena asked with a big smile.

'Oh, I do,' Theo confirmed as he picked up their joined hands and dropped a kiss on her knuckles like he'd done that night up on the sundeck. The slight rounding of her eyes told him she remembered it too. 'I absolutely do.'

* * *

An hour later, Tiffany was crawling into Theo's king-sized bed in her baggy sleep shirt and pulling the sheet up to her chin. It had been a whirlwind of a day, from her fantasy shopping spree to the massive ring she wore on her finger to the meal they'd all just shared to the crew who'd thought the whole situation was hilarious, cheekily bowing and curtsying to her when she'd gone to thank them for dinner.

But as she waited for Theo to emerge from the bathroom, it felt like it was only just beginning. Desperately she wished she was up on deck working on her book, but she couldn't risk being caught should either of their guests wander up because it was the one thing she didn't want to share.

Theo knowing had been anomaly enough.

She could do it in bed, she supposed, but she doubted she'd be able to concentrate on anything other than Theo sleeping on the couch not three metres away.

The door opened, and Tiffany startled a little as the bathroom light went out and the suite plunged into darkness momentarily before the lamp sitting on the table next to the couch snapped on to reveal Theo in a pair of clingy cotton boxer briefs and nothing else.

Helplessly, her gaze was drawn to the acres of smooth bronzed flesh of his back and shoulders and the dark hair furring his forearms, perfectly muscled legs and chest. Her nipples remembered how good it had felt having that hair rubbing against their taut peaks, and they tingled wantonly in recognition.

'That was a risky move talking about Angelika,' he said as he sorted through the pile of pillows and bedding he'd dumped on the couch before he'd used the bathroom.

Tiffany blinked. It wasn't accusatory, but she hadn't been prepared for it, either. She didn't know what she'd thought

they'd talk about – no talking at all would have been her prefer-
ence – but it wasn't this.

It did however help abruptly extinguish the mad tingle of
her nipples. 'Well, he... brought her up and I thought it would
demonstrate how well we knew each other. That you'd
confided in me about it. I thought it would seem authentic that
I knew something deeply personal about you. I'm sorry, should
I... not have?' Was he angry that she had? 'I think it went down
well?'

Nodding, he glanced at her over his shoulder briefly before
he turned back to choosing a pillow. 'It did,' he agreed. 'Thanks.
I think the old curmudgeon is finally ready to move on.'

It was said with affection – almost – as Theo plumped a
pillow before tossing it on the couch. Sitting, he swung his legs
onto the cushions and wriggled down, raising his knees to fit his
long frame into the much shorter space.

Reaching behind him, he flicked out the lamp and the room
was dark once again. But she could hear him wriggling as her
eyes adjusted to the night and she almost opened her mouth to
invite him to share the bed. It was his bed after all, and they had
shared one before.

There just hadn't been a lot of sleeping going on.

Which was precisely her concern if a mostly naked Theo was
within easy reach.

Sure, he had the dare to keep him in check, but there was
nothing to say *she* couldn't use his body to get off...

And there went her nipples again.

Now her eyes had adjusted, Tiffany kept her gaze fixed on
the ceiling, excruciatingly aware of Theo's mostly naked form
dominating the couch in her peripheral vision. All she had to do
was turn her head to get the full frontal.

'Thank you for tonight. It really did go well.' His voice was quiet, but she felt every word like he'd puffed them across her aching nipples.

'They're nice people,' she murmured. Maybe Dimitri had been a bit of a hardass to Theo, but he didn't come across as a tyrant. 'I felt sorry for them. About not being able to have kids. They both still seem so sad about it all these years later.'

'Yeah.'

'I hope you don't mind I lumbered you with three future children.'

He chuckled and this time it was a low whorl of air that kissed her nipples, following through with a swipe of a hot, wet tongue. Tiffany squeezed her legs together to stop the tingle from taking hold between her thighs.

'As long as you don't mind that I had a vasectomy when I was twenty-two and can't possibly provide them for you.'

Tiffany blinked at the startling admission. *What. The. Hell?* Her brain scrambled as she tried to compute the information. She'd never been overly maternal herself and didn't really know how she felt about having babies, but she'd have never done anything to make sure it wouldn't happen. To take such a consequential decision at such an early age rendered her speechless.

What if she met the one and changed her mind?

If she hadn't known it before, it was patently obvious now – Theo was deadly serious about never having anything more than a one-night thing. She'd assumed that, despite his convictions, Theo would one day find his one and change his ways. Now she wasn't so sure.

'Did I shock you?' he asked into the growing silence. 'This is why I don't tell people. In fact, you're the first person I've ever told. But as we were talking about fake future babies, it seemed appropriate.'

Maybe she was supposed to feel privileged or special or

something that he'd confided in her, but Tiffany just felt conflicted. It was none of her business but that didn't stop the squall of emotion in the pit of her stomach or the sudden urge to march across the space between the bed and the couch and hit him across the head with a pillow.

'No, you didn't. I mean, I'm... surprised for sure, but it's not my business.'

'It's just... I didn't ever want to be caught out, if other contraception failed,' he said as if, her business or not, he wanted her to understand such a final decision.

'You don't have to explain to me.'

He really didn't. But it did explain why, despite spreading his seed every-freaking-where, there weren't any little oopsy-daisy Theos out there in the world. Because, had there been, Tiffany had no doubt the tabloids would have sniffed them out.

There was a long pause before he spoke again. 'Do you want kids?'

It was bizarre to be talking about the topic of future children with her fake fiancé – a Greek billionaire – in his luxurious master suite on his multi-million-dollar superyacht. But this whole day had been bizarre so, why not?

'I... don't know how I feel. I can't see it happening any time soon but I'm not against the idea either. I certainly want to keep my options open.'

'That's fair.' His voice was evenly modulated and reasonable. 'But I do know how I feel.'

'How you feel *now*,' she murmured.

'I'm pretty sure it's how I'm always going to feel.'

'And you've never in your life changed your mind about something?'

'Rarely.'

His voice was laced with a grim kind of determination, and it was a visceral reminder that Theo Callisthenes was a man who knew his own mind. 'It's just so... final,' she said. 'Did you not grapple with that?'

'No. Never.'

'And what about if the unimaginable happens and you fall for someone?'

Tiffany's breath caught at the thought. What would it be like to have this man's intense, singular focus? Because something told her that if Theo ever did fall, he'd fall hard. After all, she'd had his focus for one night and hadn't been able to get it out of her head.

An even longer pause followed, and Tiffany wished she was looking at him so she could read his eyes.

'It hasn't so far.'

His soft denial was like a small jolt of electricity searing a pathway through her chest, leaving the tight ache of a burn in its wake. 'Humour me,' she said, her voice threaded with irritation at his certainty and her confusion as to why in hell this mattered to her at all.

'I suppose in that... unlikely event, if we decided we wanted to have a baby together, then I would go for a reversal.'

His confidence in such a procedure that had variable success rates bordered on arrogant. But then, that was Theo Callisthenes to the core. Expecting everything to just bend to his will. Even the re-joining of his scarred vas deferens!

'I just can't see it ever coming to that.'

Tiffany gritted her teeth. She'd officially moved from irritated to pissed. 'Are you never unsure of yourself?'

'Nope.'

Damn arrogant man. Tiffany had been leading her own life for a long time and making decisions and taking risks, but she'd never been absolutely sure they were the right ones. 'You know that's exceptionally annoying, right?'

He chuckled, and she shivered from her toes to the slick heat between her legs to her aching nipples, reminding her of how sure he'd been with her. How masterfully he'd played her body.

'I have been told, yes.'

Of course he had. 'I'm going to sleep now,' she announced grumpily, turning on her side so her back was to the couch.

Another chuckle slid into a silky, '*Kalinyhta*, Tiffany.'

'*Kalinyhta*, Theo.'

Not that Tiffany thought for a moment she was going to sleep.

16

Theo slipped out early the next morning, careful not to wake Tiffany, who was sleeping soundly after he'd heard her tossing and turning for what had felt like most of the night. He was careful to also not let his gaze linger on the back of a bare thigh and the curve of a gloriously soft ass cheek that had been exposed as she slept.

The urge to bite all the way up that thigh to that cheek then slide his tongue between her legs rode him so hard as he departed, he still had the hard-on ten minutes later as he sipped at the thick cup of Greek coffee he'd made himself at the bar.

At just before six, the sky was soft with pale pink light, but no one was up yet, either on deck or on Hydra, except for a lone fisherman. He waved to Theo as his small tin boat full of nets cut quietly through the harbour on his way out to his secret fishing spot.

Theo yawned and stretched his neck from side to side as he propped his foot on the middle railing. He'd barely slept last night either, weirdly attuned to every movement coming from the bed. Of course, the cramped confines of the couch hadn't helped. In fact, after several hours he'd given up and thrown his pillow on the plush carpet of the floor, which had been marginally better.

His neck and back bitched at him as he wondered how pissed off they'd be after a second night on the floor.

Maybe it was his divine punishment. For unleashing this façade in the first place. Or for being so grimly determined to deflect her enquiries about his vasectomy.

Her *are you never unsure of yourself* ate at him now. Because the truth was, he never had been. His decisions – both business and personal – always came after a process of deliberate enquiry where all the facts were parsed and all the pros and cons explored. So he was always absolutely confident of what he had to do to get what he wanted.

And he'd never regretted any of them. Until she'd shown up in his life.

As he'd lain there in the dark after an evening he hadn't expected to enjoy but had, – thanks to Tiffany – his easy decision to have a vasectomy all those years ago was suddenly cast in doubt.

She'd asked him what would happen if he fell for someone, and for the first time, it was a question that had caused him pause.

It hasn't so far.

The words had felt awkward coming out of his mouth and had sounded wrong going in his ears. More than that, he got the feeling that she'd been disappointed in his answer. And that, along with the uncomfortable conditions, had played on his mind all night because maybe it wasn't actually true any more.

And if so, what the hell had happened?

His phone rang and he pulled it out of his pocket. Ari. The

last time his brother had called before six it had been to tell him that his beloved wife had been killed in a car accident.

Frowning at the screen, Theo stabbed his finger at the answer button.

'Everything okay?' he demanded, not bothering with pleasantries. 'Why are you ringing this early? Is it the baby?'

His gruff concerns were greeted with a chuckle. '*Halará*, Theo. Everything is fine.'

At his brother's tone, Theo did as Ari suggested and relaxed, his grip on the coffee cup loosening. 'Did you wet the bed?'

Another chuckle. 'No, but I think Dimitri did.'

'He called you?'

'Just to let me know that things are going swimmingly. And that he'll be signing the contract when he gets back to Athens in a few days.'

'Yeah?' Theo grinned as a surge of relief took hold. Thank God. Dimitri's company would be saved and their grandfather would be very happy. 'That's fantastic.'

'Yes. I thought so. I'll message you when the deal is inked.'

Theo nodded. 'Excellent.'

'Dimitri tells me you have a fiancée now?'

Theo rolled his eyes. Great. Trust Dimitri to be an old gossip. 'Oh. Yes.' He cleared his throat. 'That.'

'Yes,' Ari repeated. 'That. Damn it, Theo. I said be on your best behaviour. Not lose your mind.'

Keeping his voice low, Theo scanned for any signs of Dimitri rattling around. 'You said it was up to me to convince him, and a fiancée was a sure-fire way of doing it. And it's worked a treat. It was inspired.'

'To Tiff? Jesus, Theo, Kelsey's going to be super pissed.'

'At you?' He snorted. Fat chance. That woman doted on him. 'Not my problem.'

'No, *malaka*. At you.'

Okay, well, that was different. Just because Kelsey had a soft spot for him didn't mean he wanted to test it. 'It made sense. We had a prior... connection and she was already on the *Nerida*. Plus, she was fine with helping.'

'Just like that, huh? Just agreed to help you.' Ari's voice dripped with sarcasm. 'With no persuasion or incentive?'

'Well... I may have offered to give her brother a leg up into the European art world.'

Ari sighed. 'Of course you did.'

'What? He's really good. I wouldn't have offered otherwise. Plus, there's nothing wrong with some quid pro quo.'

'Sure, but I doubt Kelsey will see it that way. If Tiff gets hurt in all this, she'll probably insist I have you murdered, and I'll do it because I am an excellent husband.'

Theo rolled his eyes at his brother's hyperbole and Kelsey thinking Tiffany needed any kind of protection. He'd never met a woman more self-reliant. 'She's not going to get hurt. She knows the score here. It's just for show. Just for Dimitri.'

'And what about you?' Ari asked. 'Do you know the score? Because it seems to me you're crossing a lot of lines you've never crossed before. What if you get hurt?'

Laughter cascaded from Theo's mouth even if he was touched by his brother's concern. For all their smack talk, they were close and there wasn't anything they wouldn't do for each other. 'No one's getting hurt. It's two days then everything's back to normal.'

But even as he said the words, his skin itched. Could things ever truly get back to normal when she had another month on the *Nerida* and she was back below deck as the second stew? And he was left with her perfume on his sheets and visions of that sexy ass cheek taunting him as he fell asleep in the bed where she'd lain for two nights?

Another sigh from Ari. 'If you say so.' Which, unsurprisingly, wasn't terribly comforting. 'What are you going to do about keeping Dimitri quiet?'

Theo laughed. 'You want me to feed him to the fishes?'

'I'm being serious, Theo.'

'You're overreacting. It's not like they court the paparazzi or either of them are on social media.'

'No, but he has a phone. Are you ready to explain to Pappou that you're engaged?'

Well, fuck. Ari made a good point. That was the last thing he wanted. This fake scenario needed to stay contained to the boat. 'Fine. I'll talk with him about keeping it under his hat.'

'Thank you. And just... be careful, okay? You're in unchartered waters, brother. Mind the rocks.'

Theo opened his mouth to assure Ari once more, but the phone cut off in his ear. He only wished Ari's words of warning were as easily cut off. Prior to knowing Tiffany, Theo would have had no problems dismissing them. But they resonated a little too closely now.

And the strangest part? Theo was weirdly unconcerned.

* * *

Over breakfast, Theo managed to extract a promise from Dimitri to keep their news quiet for the moment. Theo had assured him once they were back from Crete in two weeks they'd work on making a public announcement, but explained that he wanted that time with his new fiancée without becoming the paparazzi's number one target.

Given Theo's history with the paparazzi, Dimitri understood

that the first pics of the happy couple would be highly coveted and was immediately contrite about spilling the beans to Ari. Helena, frowning at her husband in disapproval, said she would ensure Dimitri kept his mouth shut.

Theo felt slightly guilty knowing that there wouldn't be an announcement and, with the deal already signed, Dimitri would have no legal recourse. But he'd cross that bridge when he got to it.

After that awkwardness, the day flew by. Between wandering around Hydra and enjoying lunch in a taverna with Dimitri and Helena and some more afternoon cruising followed by an impromptu fishing session during which they'd all caught a fish, it was dinner time before he knew it.

Maria had prepared their freshly caught fish, steaming them gently in lemon and butter so that it melted in their mouths, and they were now playing a friendly game of Biriba. Tiffany hadn't heard of the popular Greek card game but, as it was similar to rummy, she picked it up quickly and, with her croupier skills, was soon wiping the floor with them.

'Theo,' Dimitri chided him, 'your fiancée is kicking your ass.'

Theo laughed. She was kicking all their asses and being utterly magnificent in the process. He supposed a less secure man might have found it an insult to his masculinity, but he just found it a huge fucking turn on.

'It's not the first time his ass has been kicked by a woman,' Tiffany said with a smile, side-eyeing him for an exaggerated moment before leaning in a little to address their guests. 'Do you want to know about the time he was given an old-lady ass-kicking?'

Helena laughed and clapped, winking at Theo as he rolled his eyes. 'We are all ears.'

She regaled them with the story then, embellishing it even

from the version that Hugo had told and, if he didn't know differently, Theo would have sworn she'd been there as a witness. Or at least been around long enough in his life to have heard it a hundred times.

Which was entirely the point.

She was legitimising their relationship more succinctly than any display of PDA, although there was that as well. Touching his forearms, sliding her palm onto his thigh, leaning into him as they'd sat together at lunch, using a paper napkin to wipe away a smudge of yoghurt on the side of his mouth. And he'd returned the favour, touching her often too, until it had felt like the most natural thing to do.

The sizzle wasn't natural though and even less so as it built with each casual caress. It was hot and exciting. Electric. His skin alive with the static of her touch, his pulse thready with the echo of it. And he knew she felt it too, by the hint of huskiness in her breath and the prickle of goosebumps erupting beneath his palm.

By the time their guests finally retired, his entire body was humming with it.

'You can use the bathroom first,' he told her as she brushed past him into the suite, the mix of fragrances from her shampoo to her perfume to the champagne forming a heady mix that made him want to push her against the door, bury his face in her neck and inhale.

Striding far away from that temptation, he toed off his shoes and socks near the couch as the door to the bathroom opened and closed. The linen and pillows from last night had been neatly folded and stacked on the left cushion by Tiffany, he assumed, as he'd told Kelly not to bother servicing the suite whilst his guests were on board.

Reaching for the pile, he sorted through it, ostensibly

deciding whether to give the couch another try or go straight for the floor but actually hyperaware of Tiffany shedding her clothes behind closed doors. Hyperaware of the thick thud of his pulse through his chest, belly and groin. Of the aching tautness of his cock just about busting through his trousers.

The door opened and he tensed as her, 'All yours,' reached him.

The bathroom, *kalavaris*. The bathroom. Not her.

Without even acknowledging her, Theo dropped whatever the hell he had in his hand and headed for the safety of a locked door, letting out a ragged breath as he stared at himself in the vanity mirror. He looked as wild as he felt and he knew he had to get himself under control before he went back out there.

Undressing briskly, he thought of the least sexy thing he knew – Ari's goddamn never-ending spreadsheets – but by the time he was down to his boxer briefs, not even the most boring thing on earth had stood his cock down.

Reaching into his underwear, he gripped the rock-hard shaft, his breath tumbling out of him in a husky rush as he palmed himself, the exquisite torture of it hollowing out his chest. And for a moment, he was tempted to do the one thing he knew would see it gone.

But no. He was not going to do that.

Not with Tiffany a few metres away on the other side of the door. Like he was some horny boy who couldn't control himself. For damn sure if he did, that load would come steaming out under significant pressure and he wasn't sure he'd be able to suppress the resultant cry of release.

So... a cold shower it was.

And it helped. Even though the temptation to take himself in hand rode him hard, he resisted and the cold water soon did the trick. But still, he was glad for the dim-lighting when he strode out of the bathroom, and he snapped the lamp off as soon as he'd tossed everything off the couch and laid himself down.

Not that he could get comfortable. His neck immediately started to twinge and he shifted several times, trying to find a position where it wouldn't hurt as much. He was about to give up and hit the floor when Tiffany's voice drifted his way.

'If you put a shirt on you can share the bed.'

Theo's heart, which had been a hard drum in his chest, skipped a beat. Then another. Did she have any idea what kind of temptation that would be putting between them? He drew in an unsteady breath. 'I never sleep with a shirt.'

He was only sleeping in briefs for her benefit.

'Humour me,' came her dry response. 'Or stay there and rub your bloody neck again all day tomorrow.'

'It's fine,' he muttered even as his neck twinged again.

He heard the sheets rustle as she sat up. 'Theo. We're both adults. We've shared a bed before and this one is huge. I promise not to leap on you.'

Theo hooted out a laugh at the dryness of her tone, pleased to have a release from the tension in his body. 'And I have a dare to uphold.'

'Right. So just get in already.'

17

An hour into her ridiculous suggestion, Tiffany was wide awake and looking down the barrel of another sleepless night. She'd made a huge mistake. The sound of his tossing and turning and concern for the state of his neck had temporarily overridden the fact she'd been getting hotter and hotter for him as the day had worn on. Every little touch and look cranked the heat between them until she was aflame with desire.

And she'd gone and invited temptation into her bed.

So now he was just there, beside her, close enough to reach if she wanted to stretch a little. And her entire body ached with the terrible, terrible torment of it. Heat had pooled low in her belly, turning everything wonderfully liquid and lax, except for a hot path of tingles that arrowed with military precision south to her clit and north to her nipples.

It turned out that it didn't matter that she was an adult as she'd assured him, because her body was acting like a hormonal teenager. Every time she moved even slightly, she was excruciatingly aware of the slipperiness between her legs and her shirt rubbing against her aching breasts, taunting the stiff tips like it was industrial-grade sandpaper instead of soft, worn cotton.

Despite telling herself she would not, she found herself taking another sneak peek of him, the planes and angles of his classic profile intensified by the shadows of the night, the whiskery growth on his jaw darker. He smelled like soap and the laundry detergent they used below deck, and it was taking all her willpower not to wriggle closer and find out just how feral it would smell on his skin with the potency of his pheromones thrown into the mix.

'Stop it.'

Tiffany started at the low growl, her pulse leaping as her head snapped back, her eyes on the ceiling again. She swallowed. 'Stop what?'

'Looking at me.'

'I'm not... I wasn't...'

It was a barefaced lie, but he didn't call her on it as his mouth settled into a grim line. Her heart rate settled from its spike as she wondered how he'd even known she'd been looking considering his eyes hadn't opened since he'd laid his head on the pillow.

She risked another quick look for confirmation, which was a big mistake as he rolled his head to the side and caught her staring, his gaze capturing hers and not letting go. 'I swear, Tiffany, I'm holding on by a thread of honour right now.'

The low rumble of his words dragged heavy fingers through the liquid centre of her, and Tiffany could no more have turned her gaze to the ceiling than she could have flown her ass to the moon. Need blazed hot blue in his eyes, but knowing he was battling his desires too was little comfort to the ache between her legs.

'Regretting it already?' he asked, lifting an eyebrow.

Tiffany didn't act coy; she didn't seek clarification – she knew what he was talking about. She should never have invited him back into his bed. 'Yeah. A little.'

His gaze drifted to her mouth then back up again. 'Why?'

Because her act of kindness/stupidity had crystallised one stunning fact. This thing between them wasn't going to go away because it was inconvenient and neither of them wanted it. It was going to have to burn out.

'I can't seem to stop wanting you,' she admitted, each word feeling as calamitous as it was liberating.

Burning this thing out with Theo sounded like the best kind of debauchery, but how long would *that* take? And where would they be after? The stakes were too high when her best friend was married to his brother and she knew she'd be seeing him on and off for the rest of her life.

'There hasn't been a single second since you stepped on this boat that I haven't wanted to drag you onto this bed and fuck you so good and so hard and so long, you'd never want to leave.'

Tiffany bit her lip to stop from moaning as a hot tide of sensation rolled from her clit to her nipples. Her on this boat? Forever? Ready to spread her legs for him, cater to his every sexual whim whenever he came calling?

Bloody hell.

Shutting her eyes, she rolled onto her side away from him. The man still had one month left to win his dare. And she wanted more from life than being Theo Callisthenes' fuck buddy. Even if right now it sounded like the sweetest deal.

Shoving a fist between her legs to soothe the gnawing ache, she breathed in steadily. 'You're on a sex ban,' she reminded him, her voice so low and ragged she barely recognised it as her own.

A hand slid onto her shoulder, and Tiffany's eyes flashed

open. 'Who said anything about sex?' he muttered as his body pressed along hers.

His lips to her nape. The front of his chest to her back. The front of his thighs curling around to spoon hers. The long hard length of his cock notching into the cleft of her ass.

'Ari never said anything about me helping someone else with their pleasure.' Hot air puffed his wicked suggestion across her skin, causing a proliferation of goosebumps from her scalp to her nipples. 'Would you like that, Tiffany?' His lips bussed her nape with each word. 'You got an itch I can scratch?'

Tiffany moaned both at the way he said her name – low and dirty – and the visual in her brain and her entire fucking body broke out in one giant itch. Her hips involuntarily pushed back, her ass rubbing against his erection.

He groaned at the action, the rumble of hot air circling from her nape to her throat. 'Have mercy, Tiffany,' he murmured, his mouth a brand on her skin. 'I only have so much resolve.'

His ragged request squeezed through her belly, and she shut her eyes as she forced herself to stop the agonising tease. For his sake. And hers.

What did she think she was doing? Had she been about to rub herself to climax on his cock? God knew she was in such a hair-trigger state she'd probably manage it in startling time.

Gah! She was losing her grip on this.

His lips pressed into the slope where her neck met her shoulder, and she whimpered at the back of her throat. 'No kissing,' she panted, panicked suddenly that she would be the one responsible for Theo losing to Ari in their stupid dare situation.

'I'm not kissing,' he murmured, his lips vibrating against her skin, driving her wild. 'I'm nuzzling. Ari didn't say anything about nuzzling.'

He nuzzled some more, his tongue licking a hot line to the

bony notches of her neck, his hand moving simultaneously from her hip to her thigh to the hem of her shirt. Tiffany's heartbeat thumped through every pulse point as his hand pushed under and began to trek back up, skimming over her underwear, her belly, her ribs to finally claim a breast, squeezing it on a groaned, 'You have magnificent tits.'

The compliment went straight to her head but was quickly lost as his fingers found the taut aching peak of her nipple and strummed. She whimpered at the sensation, and he hushed her as he swirled his finger around the tip. 'You like that, don't you?'

Tiffany swallowed, an explosion of sensations popping behind her closed eyes. 'Yes,' she admitted on a choked husky breath.

'I remember,' he said, his voice dropping a whole other octave, 'you loved it when I did this.' He pinched her nipple and Tiffany cried out at the exquisite torment of it, her hand looping behind his neck, holding on for dear life.

Her back arched involuntarily as the torment continued, a hot kick of electricity arcing from her nipple to her clit, which pulsed urgently in response. 'Yes,' he whispered, his lips brushing her ear now. 'Good girl,' he praised as she whimpered in pleasure. 'I remember you, Tiffany. I remember you.'

He did. Tiffany had always found walking the line between pleasure and pain exceptionally stimulating, and the relentless pincer was pushing all her buttons. When he released it, she gasped as the cool air blasted the hot compressed nub that was burgeoning painfully back to taut fullness.

'I know what else you like too.'

He shifted then, and Tiffany was so boneless she fell back against the mattress as he knelt between her thighs, reached under her shirt and dragged her underwear down, stripping it off one leg and leaving it dangling around the other ankle.

Pushing her shirt up to just under her chin, he exposed her to his view, his nostrils flaring as his gaze flicked to meet hers. 'I've been dreaming about this moment ever since I woke to find you gone all those months ago.'

Tiffany swallowed. She'd been dreaming about this too. Him above her, his eyes raking over her body like it was his own personal playground and he had an all-access pass.

'Spread your legs,' he commanded, blue eyes burning, the roughness of his voice thickening his accent. 'I want to look at you.'

Her mouth dry as toast, her pulse an erratic drumbeat through her ears, Tiffany did exactly as he asked, easing her legs apart, conscious that his gaze was drifting down. Down, down, down. Zeroing in on the hot, liquid slipperiness between her legs, his eyes lingering on the dampness of her inner thighs before drifting back to her core.

His eyes devoured the sight. 'You are so fucking wet,' he muttered, his voice somehow filthy and reverent at the same time.

Tiffany couldn't speak at all as he stared at her, her hands gripping the sheets as she fought the urge to roll her hips in wanton invitation. After several screamingly long moments of nothing but Theo looking at her, the thread of her patience snapped.

'Shall I start without you?' she demanded, untangling her fingers from the sheet and sliding them to her clit, which spasmed at the touch, causing her breath to hitch.

Theo snatched at her hand, reefing it away. 'Nuh uh.' His eyes blazed a warning. '*Mine*. All mine.'

At any other time, a man making such a possessive claim would have had Tiffany using several of those words she'd learned far too young on an outback cattle station, but right now she was prepared to surrender all her agency to have Theo Callisthenes looking at her pussy like it *was* his and his alone.

He lowered himself, settling on his belly between her thighs, his face hovering mere centimetres from her slick folds as he pushed her legs wider, tossing one over his shoulder. Tiffany held her breath for one beat, two, as he looked his fill again, clearly relishing the closer view before his mouth touched down.

'Ohhhh...' she moaned as his tongue swiped right up her centre straight to the hard bullet of her clit, sending spirals of pleasure along muscle fibres that tightened deep inside her belly. And when his hands smoothed up her body to each claim a breast, his fingers pincering the nipples simultaneously, it wrenched a guttural *fuuuck* from her throat.

Tiffany felt like she was falling and flying at the same time, and she ploughed the fingers of one hand into his hair and twisted, holding him there as he wreaked havoc, desperately needing a connection to keep her grounded.

If it hurt – and it must have hurt – he didn't mention. He just hummed appreciatively as he licked and sucked, swirled and lashed, all while he squeezed and released her nipples in rhythmic pulses, catapulting Tiffany so quickly and thoroughly to orgasm it felt like he'd rewired her entire brain.

'Theo,' she cried out, her back arching as the building wave morphed in a flash from a pinprick of light into a starburst of sensation, hurtling her through a cosmic vortex of pleasure that swirled and spun and twisted, bucking through her body in ripples that intensified until she was moaning and thrashing against the bed.

His elbows clamped tight around her hips, keeping her in place as his relentless tongue drove her orgasm right to the edge of her consciousness where everything was hazy and indistinct before it started to fade, and he gentled his stimulus to long lazy swipes of his tongue and light swirling caresses around her nipples that eased her back to earth.

Tiffany was panting hard, her pulse still a water hammer through her system as she slowly came back to herself and her surroundings. She was aware of her fingers still twisted in the silken strands of his hair, the weight of her leg still thrown over his shoulder and the warmth of his breath as he nuzzled her inner thighs.

'Hey,' he murmured, his lips bussing the sensitive flesh. 'How you doing up there?'

Tiffany gave a half laugh as she raised her head off the bed, and he looked up, their gazes meeting over the top of her still-quivering body. 'I think I just touched the face of God.'

Theo chuckled a very smug chuckle. She knew the man's ego didn't need any more compliments, but it had been a transcendent experience, and she believed in giving credit where credit was due. 'You're welcome.' He grinned as he withdrew his hands, dragging her shirt down with him. Easing her leg from his shoulder, he nuzzled his way back up her body, resuming his position behind her as he slid an arm around her waist and spooned her close.

He was still hard as a rock, his erection settling between the cleft of her buttocks, prodding Tiffany out of her post-orgasmic glow.

That had to hurt.

She rocked back against him, smiling to herself as he groaned and tightened his arms around her. She did it again and his low, 'Stop that,' made her smile harder.

'I can return the favour,' she suggested, hormones that had been drunk on satiation seconds ago perking up again.

'Sex ban,' he grunted.

'No rules against blow jobs,' she reminded him, rocking again.

'Yeah... but I know how you and me work. If you so much as breathe on my cock I'm going to want to sink inside that pussy I just ate out.'

Tiffany drew in a ragged breath at the startling visual. She wasn't smiling any more because, bloody hell – she wanted him sinking into her, too.

'Now, quit moving and go to sleep,' he ordered.

Sleep? He had to be joking. With his admission over how little control he felt around her? And the echo of her orgasm still glowing in all her pleasure receptors? And another kind of glow, a different kind. In her chest. Glowing away at how good it felt to sleep with him cocooned around her like this. How right.

But surprisingly, she did sleep.

Within minutes of closing her eyes, Tiffany fell headlong into the deepest, darkest, most incredible sleep of her life.

18

Theo also slept. When his erection finally quit, anyway. Or maybe he'd drifted off before that. Given he'd woken to more wood, he couldn't be sure if he'd actually fallen asleep with it still hanging around and it was the same damn one or another one entirely.

His balls sure as hell ached like he'd been in a heightened sexual state all night.

Hardly surprising with Tiffany plastered to him like shrink wrap. At some point, he'd rolled onto his back and she'd turned, snuggling into his side, an arm draped across his chest, her thigh against his crotch.

He could also still smell her on him, taste her, which probably didn't help.

When she'd invited him to share the bed, he'd been determined that he was shutting his eyes and going to sleep. And he had tried. He had shut his eyes. But he'd been super attuned to her furtive glances in his direction, and they'd played havoc with his self-control.

He'd felt every single time she'd looked his way. The heat of it on his face and the brush of it on his chest and the intensity of it all the way down to his balls.

And when she'd admitted she couldn't stop wanting him, the words had grabbed fistfuls of his intestine and squeezed.

It had only been her turning her back on him, reminding him of that fucking dare, that had kept him in check. But still, he hadn't been able to resist touching her and if getting her off was the only way he could stick within the parameters of the dare, then he'd been up for that, because not touching her had proven impossible.

And *Christe*, she was so fucking wet. For him. Slick with desire that had filled his nostrils and had tasted rich and salty on his tongue and driven him half mad with wanting her. And way she'd keened his name as she'd come...

He hadn't just felt that physically, he'd felt it wrapping around his heart – calling to his heart. He could still feel it now as a vague kind of constriction that made it a little hard to breathe when he looked at her. Like a prickly vine slowly encircling the beating centre of him, cinching tighter as it embedded into the flesh.

Which was ridiculously fanciful and if he didn't get off the bed now, he may well take advantage of her warm body draped softly and pliantly against the taut ache of his.

She stirred and murmured something unintelligible as he eased away, and Theo froze, hoping she wouldn't wake, because he wasn't sure he'd say no if she repeated her offer of help with his erection this morning. Thankfully, her eyes stayed closed and Theo slipped out of the bed for the bathroom, thanking God and Calvin Klein for tight underwear keeping his cock from bobbing out like a fucking divining rod as he walked.

When he got to the ensuite, he knew he had to do something about it if he had any hope of getting through the rest of the day playing tour guide to Dimitri and Helena with Tiffany beside him, her taste still on his tongue. He'd fought the urge to masturbate last night but that was before he'd buried his face between her thighs and made her *touch the face of God.*

Yes, Tiffany was still only a door away and his lack of control was infuriatingly juvenile, but it was release or blow a gasket.

Peeling his underwear down and shrugging out of the shirt she'd made him put on – which had clearly failed in its duty to keep them from each other – he stepped into the shower. A warm one this time but still, he hissed out a breath as the teeming spray hit his shaft, making it buck and ache, his balls contracting painfully at the stimulus.

The luxury of the gilt-edged black tiles didn't even register as he wrapped his fingers around his shaft, biting back a groan as he fisted himself. His heart was a hard thump in his chest as he gave a light pull, the sensation almost driving him to his knees, stealing the breath from his lungs.

Groping for the tiles in front of him, Theo flattened his palm up high near where the shower head fixed to the wall, leaning heavily into it as he locked his thighs and dropped his head, the spray now hitting between his shoulder blades and running down his back.

Christe! Had he ever been this worked up in his life?

Gritting his teeth, he resolved to get it done – without thinking about Tiffany. About her crying out his name last night. Or how her heel had drummed against his back as she'd bucked through her orgasm. Or how her taste and her smell had been an intoxicating combination.

She wasn't some convenient masturbatory aid, especially given she was asleep in his bed on the other side of the bathroom door. And perhaps it was that making it difficult. Because despite the ache in his balls, it felt furtive and sleezy and he slapped the wall in frustration as he tried and failed to find a rhythm.

'Do you need a hand with that?'

Theo's head snapped up, his eyes flew open, and his hand released its loaded cargo as he looked over his shoulder to find Tiffany standing in the opening of the glass partition – no door on this fancy shower – that enclosed the cubicle on two sides and would have given her a full view of exactly what he'd been up to.

His hand slid from the tiles as he stepped away two paces, his shoulder blades and ass coming into contact with the side wall. Her gaze drifted to his cock, stiff and proud, the engorged head flushed and leaking as his pulse thundered through his ears and thumped through his abdomen.

It wasn't the first time Theo had masturbated in front of a woman. But it was the first time he'd been caught in the private act of it, and he wasn't sure of the script. He wasn't about to apologise for a perfectly natural activity he was doing in the privacy of his own bathroom, but he also didn't want her to think he was some kind of Neanderthal with zero impulse control.

Not that she was looking at his face at all, her eyes glued instead to his erect cock in the same way he imagined he'd stared at her wet pussy last night – with utter carnality.

Like she wanted in on the action.

The muscles in Theo's ass tightened and he swallowed as she finally dragged her eyes up, locking her gaze with his and said, 'Don't stop on my account.'

Theo almost groaned as his dick bucked at the husky request. 'Tiffany.'

Her gaze dropped briefly again before returning. 'I mean... that looks really painful.'

He let out a strangled laugh at the understatement. 'It really is.'

'So... don't stop.'

Oh. Holy. Jesus. 'Tiffany,' he said with a groan, a warning in his voice as his balls contracted even higher.

'It's not breaking your dare if I watch, right?'

No. But it might just break him. Still, she clearly wasn't about to faint in maidenly horror at catching him in the act of self-pleasure, and his problem was still sticking out there between them so... who was he to disappoint a lady?

Not that there was anything ladylike about her right now. She looked like a fucking wildling, standing there staring at him in her baggy T-shirt that had slipped off one shoulder, her loose, sleep-mussed hair falling about her face and shoulders, her mouth slightly parted.

'You like to watch, huh?'

She shrugged, a small smile fliting across her mouth. 'I like to watch you.'

Christe. That *you* killed him. That *you* made it personal. And he could no more have denied her the show than denied himself the performance. Sliding his hand to his cock, he fisted himself again, fighting the urge to shut his eyes at the involuntary shudder that quaked through his body.

'Take off your shirt,' he muttered, and he didn't care that it didn't sound like a polite request, because it wasn't.

It was a demand.

Her eyes rounded momentarily, and he wondered if she'd decline, but then she reached for the hem and yanked it up, pulling it over her head and tossing it on the floor behind as she took three steps into the cubicle and planted her ass against the glass directly opposite him, the spray hitting the six rows of tiles between them.

Theo hummed his satisfaction as he looked his fill, strands of her hair falling forward over her shoulders to brush the slopes of her bare breasts, almost reaching the puckered tips of her nipples that looked rosy red from his attention last night.

She was still in her underwear so technically there wasn't nudity, right?

Her panties were yellow with lacy panels down each side, a satiny panel between, the waistband sitting low enough to expose rounded hips curving into soft waist and the slight rise of belly that he'd peered over last night to watch her face as she'd climaxed.

A small bow sat in the middle of the waistband and the tiny diamanté winking from the centre caused him to stroke his cock a little faster as he pictured tearing that sweet-looking bow off with his bare teeth.

'Fancy a race?' she asked huskily as she watched the slide of his hand.

Theo's pulse spiked, his gaze flicking to her face to find her hazel eyes calmly meeting his like she hadn't just suggested something that completely contradicted the innocence of that damn bow. 'Race?'

'Yeah.' Her right hand moved from the glass behind to the indent of her waist. Then lower. His eyes tracked the movement as he worked his cock. 'You and me. Let's see how fast we can cross the finish line.'

Her hand paused at that tiny bow and Theo chugged out a laugh as he pumped himself a little faster. 'No contest there.' The way she was staring at his cock, he was barely holding himself in check as it was.

'Except, we have to cross together. First one to come without the other loses.'

He wanted to ask her what the prize was for winning, but

then her fingers toyed with the bow on her panties and he lost his place.

'Think you can gear down?'

Theo swallowed hard. He was pretty damn sure he'd give himself a hernia if he slowed his roll, but he'd do whatever she fucking wanted as long as her fingers kept moving.

Kept. Moving. South.

'Uh huh,' he muttered.

But, if anything, his hand picked up the pace, something she clearly clocked given how closely she was paying attention to the slide of his hand. 'Are you sure? Because you've had a head start and I'm already one up on you, so it might' – the tips of her fingers pushed beneath her waistband – 'take me a bit longer to get there.'

Shutting his eyes, it took all of Theo's self-control to slow his hand and reign in the feral impulse to stroke himself the half dozen times he needed to release the pressure that had gone from a simmer to a boil inside his testicles.

When he opened them again, she smiled at him approvingly before moving her fingers lower and lower and lower until she hit the jackpot, a low breathy moan slipping from her lips. The sight of her hand inside her underwear almost brought Theo to his knees, and for a moment the ragged shunt of their breathing rose louder than the sound of the water.

'That feel good?' he asked on a pant as he watched her fingers play beneath the satiny fabric.

'Uh huh,' she muttered, her eyes glued to the in/out thrust of his cock through the tight ring of his fist. 'What about you?'

'Oh yeah.' Theo nodded. 'So good.'

She looked at him through heavy lids. 'But how long can you hold on?'

No stranger to sex in all its forms, Theo knew the pleasure

that could result from delaying orgasm. But they'd been delaying this for a month – months, actually – and he doubted he could contain his release for much longer. If anything, the slower pace of his hand combined with the jiggle of her breasts as she fingered herself were cranking his release to a new level of urgency.

But she didn't have to know that.

'I can hold for as long as you need me to,' he bluffed.

'Really?'

The challenge in her eyes barely registered before she was taking the two paces required to bring them within touching distance then dropping to her knees.

Water cascaded over her body, over her tits and her hair, saturating her underwear in seconds. But she didn't remove her hand as she sat back on her haunches, legs deliberately parted so he could see her working herself as she looked up at him, her mouth temptingly close to the head of his cock.

Holy. Fuck. What fresh hell was this?

Theo's heart banged to a standstill as he squeezed his cock hard to stop the sudden threat of a boil over, biting down on a groan as he beat back the climax.

'I remember you, Theo,' she murmured, her voice dropping a whole octave. 'I remember you.'

Witch. Looking at him through eyelashes dripping with water droplets, throwing his words from last night back at him.

'You loved it when I did this.'

She didn't take that pretty mouth and plunge it down his shaft, like every nerve ending from his belly button down screamed for her to do.

No, she did something far, far worse.

Locking her gaze with his, she angled her head, directing her mouth to nuzzle an already painfully taut testicle. The sensation ripped right through him, agonisingly exquisite, and he had to lock his knees to stop from falling down as he groaned so loudly he was sure they'd hear it below deck.

But that was just the beginning of her assault on his self-control as she licked and laved and coaxed with her wicked tongue and her hot mouth until the testicle slowly dropped from its tight elevation and she could take it all, humming her satisfaction as she none-too-gently sucked, dragging it in, swiping her tongue around its contours before pushing it half way out again then sucking it back to continue the torment. Watching him the entire time through wet lashes, her gaze locked on his as her hand moved inside her soaked panties.

And when she was done tormenting one side, she moved to the other.

Theo's breath came in harsh gulps as he fought the build-up in his balls, squeezing his cock hard to quell the climax that threatened to burst forward, revisiting Ari's goddamn spreadsheets as she swirled electricity through his nuts. Half of him wanted to reach down and yank her up, flip her around, press her bare breasts to the cold glass as he tore off her underwear and drove into her from behind.

Teach her not to play with fire. But the other half – the masochist, he supposed – did not want her to stop.

She did relent though, her smile smug AF as she stood reminding him of the professional croupier again, cool and calm and in control despite her utterly debauched appearance. But he saw the fever in her eyes and he was done screwing around.

Herding her back until her shoulder blades and ass hit glass, which was now completely fogged, he slapped a hand near her head, flattening his palm as he pressed in close, his mouth mere millimetres from hers, his thighs caging her in, his hand working his cock so that she felt every stroke of it nudging her belly.

'Are you ready to quit messing around?' he growled, the spray of the shower drumming down his back.

She nodded as her fingers worked frantically inside her underwear. 'I'm close,' she panted as she fixed her gaze on his, her pupils dilated. 'So. Close.'

'Good,' he ground out, lowering his head and sucking a nipple into his mouth, sucking hard mostly because he knew she liked it like that. A little because he wanted to extract some payback for his tormented testicles.

She cried out at the suction, her back arching as the pressure inside him rose up. Pressure in his balls, pressure in his stomach, pressure in his head as his hand became a blur, his breathing became choppy, his pulse skipped erratically.

'Oh God, Theo. I'm... I'm...'

'Me too,' he panted around her nipple, as everything he'd been suppressing broke free and he came in a gasping rush, her nipple slipping from his mouth.

Ropes of ejaculate ripped from his balls to splatter her belly, and muscles everywhere clenched and released, clenched and released. In his ass and balls and thighs, around the base of his spine, shooting sparks all the way to the top, lighting up all the pathways between, spreading the orgasm through all the tributaries of his nervous system.

She stayed with him the entire way, her body shuddering and shaking, her forehead pressed to his shoulder, his forehead buried in her neck, breathing in each other's gasps as they rode the storm together. Holding on until long after it passed, until he could feel the water beating relentlessly at his back again and the world righted itself.

Shifting against him, she slid her hand from her panties and

Theo realised he must be heavy as he, too, unhanded himself and eased away, his legs still not feeling quite strong enough. Her hair was a wet tangle and her cheeks and chest were flushed and she looked thoroughly gratified and he wanted to his beat his chest because *he'd* done that to her.

He'd made her look like she'd forgotten her own name.

Their breathing still not quite back to normal, they stared at each other, like they didn't quite know what to say after such an intense experience. Theo knew what he wanted to do though. He wanted to kiss her. He wanted to kiss the living fuck out of her. He wanted to pick up her and take her to his bed and spend the day kissing her, kissing every inch of her.

Just kissing her. Which was an entirely new experience for him. Kissing was nice but it had always just been a step on the foreplay road, never the main act.

Until now. Until Tiffany.

Slowly, his heartbeat suddenly loud again, he lowered his mouth towards her. To hell with the stupid dare and this stupid fake engagement. But she stopped him before touchdown, lifting a trembling hand to press two fingers to his lips. Fingers that had been buried inside her pussy mere minutes ago, the heady aroma of her still clinging to them, and if he couldn't kiss her, then goddamn it, he'd have one last taste.

Keeping his eyes locked on hers, Theo opened his mouth and slowly sucked them inside, his tongue swirling just as her tongue had done to his balls. Her breath hitched as he took his time lapping up all the salty, sticky goodness before he released them with a wet *pfft*.

After a beat or two, she drew in a ragged breath, breaking their stare as she pushed off the glass, forcing Theo to take a step back. 'I'll see you at breakfast,' she murmured, before slipping out of the cubicle and grabbing a towel on her way out.

19

Tiffany wasn't sure how she got through the day after their shower session. And the session before that when Theo had proved beyond doubt he was a man who liked to eat. Over the intervening months since the wedding, she'd thought about their night together so often, she'd figured she'd somehow exaggerated how good he was at pleasuring a woman.

Romanticised the entire experience.

But nope. The man ate pussy like the ancient Greek Gods of Greed and Debauchery had sent him to earth entirely for the purpose of cunnilingus.

And she'd wanted to kiss him so bad this morning, her lips burning with the need for his mouth. It had been so freaking tempting. But they'd pushed the envelope enough and she'd known if they started, they wouldn't stop and that envelope wouldn't have just been pushed, it'd have been incinerated.

Fortunately, it was Dimitri and Helena's last day and she thanked all the Greek gods for that as they motored to Mykonos where they were dining together one last time before they parted ways.

Frankly, it couldn't come soon enough.

Because then things between her and Theo could get back to normal. Him above deck, her below. Him, an uber-wealthy, entitled playboy so commitment-phobic he'd had a vasectomy at the age of twenty-two. Her, a cruise ship croupier from an outback cattle station and wannabe author who had no intention of ever being a rich man's darling.

They just had to get through lunch.

Which, in the end, wasn't much of a hardship. The taverna was away from the Mykonos tourist traps and known and beloved by both Dimitri and Theo, who'd been greeted by several people before they'd even taken a seat.

It was obviously a family restaurant well patronised by locals, every age group sitting around rough-hewn tables bearing checked tablecloths. An area was cleared for a dance floor where little kids grooved to the traditional folk songs being played by three old guys sitting in an alcove wearing traditional Greek vests – a guitarist, a bouzouki player and a guy playing the accordion.

The atmosphere was lively rather than loud and the lamb she'd ordered and devoured had melted in her mouth. 'To the happy couple,' Dimitri said as they all raised their shot glasses of ouzo that had been delivered compliments of the house. 'It has been an absolute delight getting to know you, Tiffany.'

Dimitri smiled at her as Helena added, 'We've had a thoroughly enjoyable two days.'

Despite her wanting it over, Tiffany couldn't help but agree. Their guests had been easy-going and good company. 'I'm so pleased we had a chance to get to know one another,' she said. 'We've had a great time, haven't we, Theo?'

She knew Theo had history with Dimitri that wasn't so pleasant but, for all that, he'd seemed to enjoy having the old man around. 'Indeed,' Theo graciously agreed, his gaze lingering on hers, making Tiffany think it wasn't the company to which he was referring.

'*Yamas*,' Dimitri said as they all tapped their glasses together.

'*Yamas*,' Tiffany murmured in unison with the other three as she promptly threw back the shot, enjoying the spicy aromatics of the aniseed flavour.

Dimitri nudged Theo with a chuckle. 'This one is definitely a keeper.'

Theo laughed and said, 'Indeed,' again with a wriggle of his eyebrows.

Gesturing to the waiter, Dimitri said, 'Another, please.'

'Dimitri,' Helena chided.

'Just one more,' he coaxed, shooting his wife a smile.

Rolling her eyes, she said, 'One more. Or you'll be asleep in your supper.'

He laughed heartily as he winked at Theo. 'Never get old, Theo.' He waved the waiter over. 'It is a terrible thing.'

Considering Dimitri was relatively spry, he didn't look too heartbroken as their glasses were topped up and they all clinked again, knocking back the second shot with another round of, '*Yamas*.'

'Theo!'

Tiffany looked over her shoulder to find a man maybe ten years older than Theo approaching. He was tall and distinguished with elegant grey wings in his hair.

'Vasilis!' Theo smiled and rose from his seat and the two men hugged affectionately as they spoke in rapid-fire Greek Tiffany had no hope of picking up, before he performed the introductions, switching to English for her benefit.

'And this is Tiffany.'

'Tiffany.' Vasilis, an old friend of Theo's who apparently lived on Mykonos and was into real estate, glanced speculatively from her to him, back to her again, his gaze not missing the ring on her finger as he bowed over her hand. 'Where has he been hiding you?' he asked in accented English.

She smiled. 'On his superyacht.' Everyone laughed, but hey, it was kinda true.

'Is Deidre here?' Theo asked.

'Of course.' He pointed to a table closer to the back where a stunning woman in red chatted to two adorable girls who looked about five or six, with chocolate curls and matching floral sundresses. 'The twins are here too.'

'Gosh, they've grown,' Theo remarked.

'Time flies, my friend,' he said, slinging an arm around Theo's shoulders.

'This is just what I was telling him,' Dimitri murmured.

Vasilis opened his mouth as if to agree but stopped as the musicians started a new song, and he grinned instead. 'Tiffany.' He smiled at her. 'This is your lucky day. Nobody dances the Sirtaki like me. Theo' – he pronounced it with its full Greek inflection, the way Dimitri and Helena had done the last couple of days – 'tell her how well I dance.'

Theo laughed. 'You used to, back before you had grey hair and two little girls.'

'Some things you don't forget.' He held out his hand. 'Come.' He winked at her. 'Dance with me.'

'Oh.' Tiffany shook her head. She could shake her booty in a night club as well as the next person, but folk dancing was not her thing. 'I don't know...'

He waved away her objections. 'It's the Zorba song, everyone knows that dance.'

Tuning into the music, Tiffany realised she did recognise the tune, the slow and repetitive opening notes warbling from the bouzouki the soundtrack to so many Greek movies and television she'd watched over the years.

'Follow my lead,' he said with a wink.

Laughing, Tiffany let him tug her onto the empty dance floor. She could see people turning in their chairs to watch but was only conscious of Theo's gaze as she stood beside Vasilis, one arm straddling his shoulders, the other raised out to her side as she shifted her weight from one foot to the other, travelling a few steps one way, then back again as she followed his lead.

Theo's gaze followed her and she felt... sexy as the tempo of the song slowly picked up. Another expensive kaftan-style dress shifted and moved with her body, floating and skimming as she pushed her hair behind her ears to expose gold hoops swinging against the side of her neck.

Other people joined them, her arm straddling someone else's shoulder on the other side as a line formed and then when it didn't fit on the dance floor, it morphed into a circle, the music getting faster and faster. She laughed up at Vasilis as she fumbled the steps trying to keep up but all the time, acutely aware of Theo. Watching her.

His intense gaze a brand on her flesh that thrilled and titillated.

Then suddenly he was there, squeezing into the circle beside her, his hand sliding to her opposite shoulder, her hand sliding to his nape, instantly falling in with the tempo, smiling down at her as she smiled up at him and her heart fluttered madly, and not from exertion.

Vasilis's wife joined them too, their twin girls spinning around in the middle of the circle as the music reached its crescendo and stopped dramatically to claps and cheers. Without conscious thought, Tiffany collapsed laughing into

Theo's arms, energised and caught up in the joy and the spirit in the taverna.

'That was great,' she said, her face aching from smiling so hard as she raised her voice to be heard over the noise of the crowded dance floor.

He grinned. 'You were great.'

'She's a keeper, that one,' Vasilis teased Theo as he swung one of his daughters up in his arms.

Theo nodded, his blue eyes flirty. 'She is.'

And Tiffany's heart went *kerthunk*.

* * *

Dimitri and Helena left soon after the dancing with hints about wedding invitations, but Tiffany and Theo stayed on for a while, joining Vasilis and Deidre, indulging in another ouzo or two and relaxed, affectionate banter, and it reminded Tiffany of the time Theo's English friends had stayed on the yacht. Except perhaps even more so given the closer cultural ties between Vasilis and Theo.

The couple's curiosity about Tiffany and Theo's relationship was palpable – Deidre's gaze kept drifting to the engagement ring – and she and Theo didn't do much to tamp it down considering they could have easily dropped the act with Dimitri and Helena gone. But, high on good company and good food, on dancing and ouzo and two giggling girls who gazed at Theo adoringly, it was too easy to keep touching and flirting.

And here, in the bubble of this little local taverna, it didn't feel like an act. But perhaps that was the ouzo.

Thankfully, Deidre and Vasilis were too polite to push and Tiffany was pleased she didn't have to lie to anyone else. She was also pleased to see yet another facet of Theo's life. The one here on Mykonos, which he clearly relished as he talked about retiring here one day.

'Did you mean that?' she asked as they left the taverna later in the afternoon. 'About retiring?'

He'd been holding her hand as they'd left and it felt like the most natural thing in the world to keep doing so as they walked past whitewashed houses along cobblestoned pathways, the thick white paint between the stones making it look as if it had been crazy glued together.

'Yes,' he said with a smile. 'Absolutely. One day.'

'Kelsey says your house here is stunning.'

'It is. Even if I do say so myself.' He gave a self-deprecating laugh. 'Want to see it?'

Tiffany wasn't sure if it was because she really wanted to see it or because it would delay their inevitable return to the boat and reality, but she found herself nodding. This whole two days had been a fantasy; would it hurt to prolong it for a little longer? 'I would love to.'

'It's about a fifteen-minute walk from here.'

'Fine by me.' More than fine as he tugged her hand and she followed.

Tiffany had been to Mykonos several times already on the big cruise ships, but she'd never wandered away from the main tourist street or the bars along the water's edge. Which had clearly been a huge mistake. The labyrinth of streets wended their way up the incline, getting quieter and quieter but no less beautiful as they left the old town behind.

The scenery was stunning, from the stark white of house walls boasting pops of red and blue and yellow in their shutters and door trims as well as the vibrant pinks and purples of climbing bougainvillea and pots of colourful geraniums, to glimpses of the sparkling Aegean down laneways and around corners.

Then there was the friendly way the locals greeted Theo, like he was one of them, and their casual curiosity about her as they slid her sideways glances and tossed what was clearly ribald comments at him in rapid-fire Greek, making him laugh as they passed.

But nothing prepared her for the majesty of his villa. Its modest stone façade and yellow door gave way to the inner sanctum, her eyes adjusting from the bright sunshine outside to the darker entrance area. Thick walls made the interior blessedly cool, and Tiffany's eye was immediately drawn past the open plan layout to the far end of the house. Theo had texted someone as they'd walked to open up for him and she could see gauzy white curtains billowing in the breeze from open French doors, revealing glimpses of endless blue sky and even bluer sea.

Toeing off her sandals at the door, Tiffany followed Theo towards the light, gorgeous mosaic tiles cool beneath her bare feet. And it did not disappoint as she stepped out onto the terrace, walking past a mosaic-topped table, around the elegant curves of the infinity-edged swimming pool jutting out from the hill and on to the railing.

Sweeping her head from side to side, she took in the full one-eighty-degree view of the Aegean far below, and it was breathtaking. The sparkle of the sea. The toy-like outlines of two huge modern cruise ships at anchor completely dwarfed by the ancient vista of island and water. The random, higgledy-piggledy placement of the whitewashed houses on every side. And the famous Mykonos windmills in the distance.

'Ohhhh, Theo,' she said on a breathy sigh as she leant on the railing and stared out over the jewel-like panorama.

'You like it?'

She turned to find him standing beside her at the railing. 'It's... I don't have words.' She glanced back at the view, the light breeze ruffling through her hair and providing relief from the lingering hint of heat in the air. 'I can see why you love it so much.'

'Yeah.' He nodded. 'It's beautiful.'

But when she glanced at him, he wasn't looking at the view, he was looking at her, causing her pulse to flutter and her cheeks to warm before she quickly looked away again.

'It's inspiring,' she said, changing the topic.

Because it was he who was beautiful. The loose white linen shirt he was wearing accentuated the perfect stretch of his bronzed skin, from the way it was rolled to expose the dark hair on his ropey forearms to the V at his neck, giving a glimpse of hard chest. Dark whiskers peppered his throat and jaw, a perfect counterpoint to the jut of his forehead and the crystalline blue of his eyes.

Theo Callisthenes looked like he belonged here. On high. Dominating the terrace and the landscape around them like a god. The God of Desire and Decadence and Debauchery, and her fingers trembled as they gripped the railing a little tighter. What would it take to bring this thoroughly modern god to his knees?

'I have an idea,' he murmured, his voice low and silky.

Tiffany almost laughed out loud as she wondered if his idea was as pornographic as the ideas running through her head right now.

'Why don't I send for your laptop? It's been several days since you wrote something, and you're right.' His gaze shifted to the sea. 'It is inspiring. You can write for as long as you like. Dip in and out of the pool if it helps. I have work I can be getting on with as well. Then when you're done, we can have a late supper and go back to the boat after?'

Okay. Not pornographic. But as freaking inspired as the view. Just the suggestion of it had her fingers itching and her characters calling. How could she resist writing with all of this in front of her? When would she ever get an opportunity as amazing as this again?

Tiffany nodded as she looked at his profile. 'Yes. Thank you. That would be...' He turned his head and their gazes locked, the blue of his eyes darker now, reflecting the unfathomable blue of the sea. 'Amazing.'

He smiled. 'Excellent. Have a seat.' He gestured to the sun loungers scattered around the pool. 'I'll make a couple of calls.'

20

Despite the inspirational potential of the view, Tiffany worried that knowing Theo was just inside doing his own work would make it hard to concentrate on the story. She was wrong. Her muse thrived thanks to the panorama, words flowing like magic from her fingertips, and when they faltered, a quick peek at the view for a little stimulus and she was off again.

She wrote for several hours, stopping only when day turned to dusk to admire the changing palette of the sky. Theo must have had the same idea as he joined her at the railing, bearing two glasses of white wine, handing her one.

'*Yamas*,' he said, clinking his glass to hers, their arms brushing as the crystal-clear ring was caught by the breeze and carried away over the rooftops of Mykonos.

'*Yamas.*'

'I think this is my favourite time of day here,' he murmured as he stared at the horizon. 'I like how the softening light settles across the church domes and the colours of the sunset play across the water.'

Tiffany nodded as she sipped the cold, crisp wine. The sky, a cotton candy pink at the moment, was turning the sea a deep kind of mauve.

'My *pappou*. He likes the sunrise. When he stays here with the family, I know exactly where I'm going to find him every morning.'

She liked the way Theo's voice softened when he talked about his grandfather. His affection for him was obvious. 'It must be magnificent here during storms, too.'

'Uh huh. You can see them coming from miles away. New Year's Eve fireworks are pretty spectacular too.'

'I'll bet.' It was no wonder Kelsey had raved about this place; it truly was spectacular.

'How's the writing?'

'It's going well. I've written a few thousand words.'

He whistled as he turned his head in her direction. 'How far along are you now?'

Tiffany shrugged. 'About halfway, I reckon.'

'And how much had you written before the *Nerida*?'

Meeting his gaze, she smiled. 'None.'

Grinning like he'd personally written each word himself, he said, 'You must be happy with that.'

'Very,' she agreed, his grin turning her belly liquid and making her want to lean into him. Dragging her gaze back to the sea, she asked, 'How about your work?'

His grin turned to a grimace in her peripheral vision. 'I'm reading a bunch of reports Ari insists I read before a Zoom meeting tomorrow afternoon.'

'What are they about?'

He huffed out a breath as he released a long string of complicated-sounding Greek words which his accent somehow made sound romantic. 'Or, in English,' he translated, 'the effects of air and water quality on the control and containment of pathogens in ship galleys.'

Tiffany laughed. Okay, maybe not so romantic. 'That sounds fun,' she teased, glancing at his profile again.

'About as fun as a root canal,' he admitted with a chuckle. 'But speaking of galleys.' He caught her gaze. 'Are you hungry?'

For food? After their late lunch? Not really. For this man, standing beside her, the brush of his arm sending tiny spirals of pleasure to her breasts and belly, looking at her like he hadn't been talking about food at all – she was freaking starving.

Gah. They really should get back to the boat. But... ohhh, that view. 'A little,' she murmured as she returned her attention to the horizon. 'But I'd like to squeeze in a bit more writing?' She knew that dusk would linger for a while longer before ceding to evening and she wanted to squeeze every second out of the light if she could.

'Sounds good.' He nodded briskly, as if he understood she was trying to temper the chemistry between them, and he was determined to do the same. 'My housekeeper has dropped off freshly baked spanakopita. Why don't I bring it out in an hour and we eat out here on the terrace?'

Mmm. Spanakopita. Theo had just said the magic words. 'Yeah. That sounds good.'

'Okay.' He took a sip of his wine. 'I'll leave you to it.'

* * *

An hour later, true to his word, Theo stepped onto the terrace with a loaded tray and Tiffany shut down her document, emailed herself a copy and closed the lid on the laptop. The table was big enough for twelve, but they sat together at the end closest to the house where the kitchen bench that overlooked the terrace and contained the sink extended into the outdoor space. The long window that ran the length of the bench flipped up awning-style to allow things to be easily passed from the kitchen as well as seamlessly connecting the indoors with the out.

He regaled her with stories that made her laugh about the culinary magic of his housekeeper as they devoured her flaky, melt-in-the-mouth spanakopita and the fresh salad bursting with flavours of ripe, red tomatoes, tangy Kalamata olives and creamy burrata. Tiffany couldn't work out which smelled better – the cheesy layers of pastry, spinach and feta or Theo Callisthenes in all his ouzo and white-linen goodness.

'Another glass?' he asked as they finished the bottle of wine he'd opened earlier.

'No, thanks,' she murmured, shaking her head.

She wanted to say yes, wanted to enjoy this buzzy feeling with Theo that had little to do with the wine or the views, and pretend this was her life – but it wasn't. And she should really take off this ring and get back to the boat because the longer she stayed up here with him laughing and trading life stories in this place he loved so much, the easier it was going to be to fall for the guy, and that would be a seriously dumb thing to do.

She knew from Kelsey and Ari that Cinderella stories came true, that they did exist, that super-rich men – Callisthenes men – fell for ordinary/everyday women.

But not this Callisthenes. Not the charming playboy who, this engineered situation aside, wasn't interested in anything past one night.

She was playing a role here. So was he. For a specific purpose. Which was essentially done. And she wasn't her

mother; she didn't need money and status for security or valida-
tion. She'd already had a life rich with experiences, and now it
looked like Mikey would no longer need her financial
assistance, she could invest in herself. Find somewhere inexpen-
sive to live for a few months and finish her book without
distractions.

Monetary, occupational or human.

'We should probably get back,' she said, placing her empty
wine glass on the table.

He nodded slowly, his eyes hooded in the night. 'I'm going to
take a swim first. Care to join me?'

Tiffany almost laughed. If she got into the water with him in
that luxurious, infinity-edged pool with both of them in next to
nothing, she knew without a doubt where that would lead. 'You
know they say you shouldn't swim within an hour of having a
meal.'

He grinned as he stood, his chair legs scraping on the stones
still warm beneath their feet. 'How'd we ever fall for that?'

She did laugh this time; she couldn't help herself. 'I don't
know.'

'C'mon.' He held out his hand and twinkled his fingers. 'You
know you want to.'

Yeah, she did. God help her, she really did. The water looked
cool and inviting and Theo was just too damn tempting for
words, but she would not lose her head, or other vital pieces of
her anatomy, here tonight.

'Nope.' She stood, her chair also scraping as she pushed it
back. 'You swim, I'll do the dishes.'

A frown knitted his brows together. 'No way. You're my guest,
leave them.'

'It's not much,' she insisted. 'And it's the least I can do for the
gift of this day.' She picked up the plates. 'Go,' she said, tipping

her chin in the direction of the pool. 'It won't take me long and I'll be straight out again.'

Not giving him a chance to argue, she turned away, taking the three steps to the granite bench top and pushing the dishes through to sit beside the sink. When she turned back for more, Theo was shucking out of his clothes by the pool edge.

All of his clothes.

He was shirtless, and his bare ass was exposed as he pushed his underwear down his legs and kicked it aside, and Tiffany's throat constricted at his breathtakingly masculine silhouette. There was no moon out as of yet and with few houses nearby lit up, he was cloaked in shadow. But her eyes were already adjusted to the low light, and she could make out every line of his body.

The bulk of a calf, the muscular delineation of thigh, the globe of an ass cheek, the puckered pillow of abs, the span of a chest and the firm brace of strong shoulders. As if a classical Greek master sculptor had hewn him from the Mykonos night.

He looked over his shoulder and caught her staring. 'Are you sure?' he asked with a wicked grin.

Forcing herself to keep her eyes on his face and not how the slight twist of his body had exposed his state of semi-arousal, she masked her expression to one of cool indifference. 'Positive,' she murmured before she returned her attention to the job at hand.

His chuckle and then a splash followed her all the way inside the kitchen.

Tiffany lingered over the dishes, which was difficult considering how few there were. When they were done and the leftovers were put in the fridge and the table was wiped down, she snooped around the photographs that were strewn around the living area. All family ones, a lot of faces she recognised from the wedding. Parents and grandparents and cousins, many of them taken on the terrace outside at various stages over the years.

There was also one with his English mates outside a pub somewhere, and another black-and-white photo of a young boy and an old man in simple clothes sitting in a small tin boat loaded with nets, smiling at the camera.

His grandfather with his father perhaps?

All the faces laughed back at her from their frames, and she was struck by how happy everybody appeared. Which made her think about all the family photos that had been around her house growing up. Her and her brothers and her parents, the image of cosy family domesticity. Until her father had ruined it all in one fell swoop and the pictures had suddenly felt like fantasies framed in lies.

The memories unsettled her, chasing her outside to find Theo, his hair slicked back, his arms resting on the infinity edge, gazing down at the town below. Crossing to the railing where they'd stood earlier, she looked down too. Lights from restaurants and clubs lining the shore reflected in the water as the sound of distant music drifted up the hill.

The harbour wall was lit, as was the marina it protected, the gleaming shells of sleek expensive motorboats and yachts clearly visible. Beyond the stone walls, the lights from much smaller boats that could not be made out at this distance bobbed and twinkled their presence to all and sundry.

'Crete tomorrow,' he said, his quiet voice floating to her on the breeze, spreading goosebumps up her arms.

She nodded but didn't glance his way. 'Looking forward to it.' Even if it would be awkward AF going back to his second stew after they'd mutually masturbated in his shower just this morning.

But they'd get past it. They'd gotten past having already

spent a debauched night together when she'd first joined the crew – they'd manage this, too. And it was only for another month. Tiffany had once put up with sharing a bunk with a woman who ate her own toenail clippings – she could certainly put up with the very easy-on-the eyes Theo Callisthenes for one lousy month.

'You're quiet,' he observed. 'Everything okay?'

She turned her head to find him watching her, concern wrinkling his brow, and her heart did a funny little giddy-up in her chest as she immediately doubted her previous assertion. 'Yup.' She returned her gaze to the dance of lights, which seem to suddenly blur, and she realised her eyes were a little misty.

Damn it, when had the man become so bloody attuned to the nuances of her body language? Was it not enough that he was hot AF?

Gripping the railing, she blinked rapidly, the swish of water barely penetrating her consciousness until he rose from the pool like Poseidon in her peripheral vision, pushing himself up onto the sandstone edging with a bulge of biceps, water sluicing off him as he stood. Even then she didn't turn to face him, sparing her frontal lobe his full frontal but conscious of him crossing behind her to where he'd left two towels earlier and then conscious of his footsteps coming closer.

His hands slid onto her upper arms first, his body slotting in behind hers a beat after. He didn't press himself against her or pull her into him; he just stood there, a solid wall of heat as he said, 'Tiffany?' It was low and soft, and she shut her eyes against the tug of sympathy. 'What's wrong?'

'It's nothing.'

'You seem... sad.'

Oh, come on. Emotional intelligence now? Why was he being all the things she needed from a man that she *couldn't* need from *him*? 'I was just... looking at your family photos. You all seem very close-knit.'

'Ah.'

That was it. Just ah. But it was an ah that spoke volumes about his level of understanding. His arms, still glistening with water droplets, slipped around her shoulders then and he did pull her gently to him, wrapping her up. Tiffany could feel the dampness of his bare skin on her nape as he tucked her head under his chin and she squeezed her eyes shut, relaxing into his solid embrace.

'It's stupid,' she said huskily, surprised by the emotional impact of Theo's family photos.

Where had that come from? Was it because he was the only man she'd ever told about her complicated history with her family? Or because it had been a perfect day and she'd been surrounded by all the beauty in Theo's full life? Was it this stark contrast to her own more solitary existence, that made her especially vulnerable to his quiet empathy?

'Shh,' he whispered. 'It's okay.'

And it felt okay as she stood there quietly in the circle of his arms, no need for words, just staring into the night, his body gently swaying. Back and forth, soothing the raw emotion that had launched a stealth attack, blunting its sharp edges and tamping it back down until she didn't feel like crying any more.

She felt like forgetting.

Like obliterating this episode of vulnerability from her memory banks. She hated how being vulnerable made her feel. Like she was that twelve-year-old kid again walking in on her dad and the neighbour's wife, realising her life would never be the same.

So she chose oblivion. And she'd take it in the form of an orgasm. But not just any orgasm, because she could go inside right now and bang one out. An orgasm with a man who not only knew what he was doing but who'd figure out damn quickly why and do it anyway because for reasons neither she, nor she suspected he, wanted to examine too closely, they were already something more to each other than a one-and-done.

Healthy? No. But right now it felt necessary.

21

Tiffany's pulse slugged hot through her system as she slowly, subtlety, also began to sway. But not with his rhythm – against it. So her ass brushed against his cock one way and then the other in complete counterbalance to his direction.

She sensed the moment Theo clocked the change. His arms tightened a little, the muscles of his chest and abdomen tensed at her back, his sway faltered momentarily as if he wasn't quite sure her movements were accidental or just plain provocative.

So she made it damn clear it was the latter as she rotated her ass in a deliberate movement against his cock, which was already fully clued in to her intent.

'Tiffany?' His voice was rough, his breath warm as it brushed her temple.

'Could you just...' She slid her hands to his forearms, which had dried in the light breeze, and gently tugged them apart, sliding her hands to his to redirect them. 'Could you just...' she repeated, guiding his palms to her breasts and whimpering as he cupped the aching flesh. 'Oh God, yes.' Her head flopped back into the crook of his neck. 'That,' she muttered. 'Like that.'

'Tiffany.'

'Please,' she whispered, turning her head so her cheek rubbed his throat, the delicious prick of his stubble sending a shudder of ecstasy coursing through her body. 'I need...' She swallowed, her throat parched as desire and grief segued into a feral kind of lust.

'It's okay.' His breath was hot in her ear as he met her ass rub with a full-on grind that caused her to gasp. 'I know what you need.'

Her pulse tripped as his fingers found her stiff nipples through the fabric of her dress and bra and squeezed. And *fuuuck* he did know. The sensation lanced her straight down to her core and she moaned in guttural satisfaction as she reached between them, frantically gathering her dress with fingers that trembled to the point of uselessness as she tried to slide it up and out of the way.

Because she didn't just need an orgasm, she realised. She needed more than that. She needed him in her, she needed the oblivion of possession.

His possession. The way she knew only he could deliver.

Her frantic pulse drove the all-consuming need, her fingers brushing against the steel of his shaft, which was barely contained by the towel he was wearing, and he muttered, '*Theé dóse mou dýnami.*'

Tiffany had no idea what that meant, but it sounded like an entreaty. Which was hot AF. She liked that she could make him feel as reckless and as helpless as she was feeling.

Grabbing for the towel next, her fingers found the knot where it was fastened low around his hips and pulled, satisfied when it fell to the ground. Her hand slid onto the taut drum of his cock and she panted, 'Oh yes,' as she palmed him and said, 'Please. I need you. In me. Now.'

She didn't care that they were standing in the open where possibly every one of his neighbours could watch the show; all she cared about was having Theo inside her, like that first night when he'd ruined her for all other men.

'Wait.' He grabbed her around the wrist, stilling the movement.

He flipped her in his arms, his eyes flaring a hot blue flame into hers as his bare chest heaved, and he used both hands to manacle her wrists behind her back now as she struggled against his restraint.

'You want me to fuck you, Tiffany?' he growled, his voice dark as pitch, his wet slicked-back hair giving him an almost devilish edge.

She almost moaned out loud at his deliberate use of both profanity and her name. 'Yes,' she panted. All she could think about was him between her legs.

Owning her.

His jaw clenched as his fingers tightened around her wrists. 'Even if that means I break my pact with my brother?' he ground out.

Which was the bucket of cold water her libido didn't – or perhaps did – need right now.

Tiffany's lust-addled brain grappled with the words coming out of his mouth. His mouth that was close enough to kiss. Which would also be violating the parameters of that bloody stupid dare. She shut her eyes on a ragged breath, her wrists halting their twisting.

'I'm sorry.' Her lids opened to find him staring at her mouth like he was barely stopping himself from devouring it with his own.

Yet he was proving himself much more in control than she was at the moment.

'You're right. It's not fair of me to ask. I guess I just' – she shook her head, silently castigating herself for being so needy as she battled to normalise her pulse and breathing – 'forgot for a moment that this isn't real.'

'Yeah.' He nodded, also still satisfyingly out of breath. 'We've kinda blurred the lines the past two days, haven't we?'

She gave a self-deprecating laugh. 'You can say that again. Especially coming to Mykonos. Meeting your friends and seeing the villa, doing some writing here, seeing pictures of your family... I guess I got swept up in the fantasy of it all.'

'You did, huh?'

Tiffany couldn't believe she'd let it all affect her so much. 'Stupid, right?'

'No.' His eyes glowed blue in the night, capturing hers as his hands came up to cup her jaw, his unsteady breath puffing currents of warm air on her face. 'Unless that makes me stupid, too.'

Her heart thumped at his surprising admission. So... he'd lost track of reality, too?

What did that even mean?

But there was no time for analysis as his expression morphed before her eyes, transforming his demeanour. She watched as Theo stepped right over the mental hurdle of the dare he'd accepted from Ari and left it behind in the dust as his mouth crashed down on hers.

Tiffany was officially lost as he stole her breath and plundered her mouth like the pirate she'd fancied him to be, taking instant control. Short, hard kisses. Long, deep, drugging kisses. Kisses where he used his tongue to devastating effect, teasing the seam of her lips, probing the recesses of her mouth, encouraging her tongue in a reciprocal dance that had her clinging and gasping and whimpering for more. Her head spun with the intoxication of it all, the harsh suck of his breath and the feral edge to his groans dizzying her so much she had to cling to his shoulders just to stay upright.

God, she'd missed this. Missed the way he'd kissed her so masterfully that first night.

When he eventually wrenched his mouth from hers, he muttered, 'Wrap your legs around me and hold on.'

She barely registered the instructions before he was lifting her, but she caught on fast, winding her legs around his waist as he carried her to the table and deposited her there. It was a little more secluded compared to the railing, but only just.

Stepping between her legs, he claimed the space as his own, kissing her again, his hands sliding to cradle her face, angling her mouth exactly where he wanted it. But he wasn't exactly where she wanted him and now he'd broken her from the intensity of their railing kiss, Tiffany was able to think again.

To become impatient again. To be greedy again.

Reaching between them, she slid her hand onto the silky hard steel of his cock, her thumb smearing the fluid already leaking from the slit, and he broke the kiss on a groan, his forehead pressed to hers. 'Now,' she demanded as she pulled at the hem of her dress once again, getting it high enough to align him with her core.

'Off,' he panted, puffing hot air on her face as he plucked at the dress.

'No.' Tiffany shook her head, relishing being back in control. 'Like this.' Because there was something deliciously exhibitionist about him being naked and very definitely feral about her being fully clothed, the idea of it speeding up a pulse already thumping erratically.

His gaze met the challenge in hers and there was nothing but the combined pant of their breathing for a beat or two before he reached for one side of her panties and ripped. Then repeated it on the other side.

And fuck if that didn't almost make her come on the spot.

'I have condoms in the house,' he muttered as he yanked the tattered fabric out from under her and tossed it over his shoulder.

They'd used condoms that first night but given he'd had a vasectomy and they'd already talked prior to their first time about their fastidious measures with their sexual health, Tiffany didn't want to wait a second longer. 'I'm okay without. If you are?'

He didn't reply, just locked his gaze with hers as he pulled her hips to the edge of the table. Her dress slipped off one shoulder as he guided himself to her slick entrance, the thick nudge of his head notching briefly before he plunged inside on a grunt.

Tiffany cried out at the perfect utter savageness of it, seeing stars. Real ones and the ones that popped and fizzed behind eyelids when the pleasure was so intense it forked like lightning everywhere.

'You okay?' he panted.

Forcing her eyes open, she nodded. 'Yes. God, yes.' She slid an arm around his neck, her fingers pushing into the damp hair at his nape, and she captured his gaze. 'Exactly like that. Don't stop.'

Planting his knuckles either side of her thighs on the table-top, he followed her instructions to the letter, hunching over her with every thrust, his forehead pressed to her bare shoulder as he drove in and out with an intensity that was wholly uncivilised. An intensity that wiped her mind of anything other than the orgasm that screamed out at her with such rabid force, the powerful contractions of her pussy dragged Theo into the maelstrom with her, crying out his own release as he bucked and grinded into her over and over and over until neither of them had anything to left to give.

It took an eon for Tiffany to drift back to earth, but they didn't talk after. Theo just picked her up, and she held on bonelessly as he strode into a bedroom and then into a bathroom and a shower cubicle, stripped her out of her clothes, turned on the spray, stepped into it with her and started all over again.

Theo woke to an empty bed and a flood of bright sunshine through the large window overlooking the terrace. It bounced off the white sheets, the whitewashed walls and the gauzy white curtains, which were more romantic than practical.

He spotted Tiffany at the railing, staring out at the sparkling panorama, the hem of the dress she'd worn yesterday fluttering around her calves in the breeze, tendrils of hair that had escaped her high messy bun blowing around her nape. And just seeing her there felt like sunbeams in his chest.

His villa had been enthusiastically lauded by anybody who had ever visited, but her quiet, breathy '*Ohhh Theo,*' and her inability to find adequate words for it, had meant more than any hyperbolic praise.

Because that was exactly how he felt about his home.

And Mykonos. The island was such an integral part of him it was impossible to define. And her genuine pleasure in all its quaintness and quirks had spoken to him as they'd walked to his place yesterday. Her enthusiastic appreciation for the authenticity of the island, beyond the touristy flash of Chora, had been refreshing.

Other women he'd brought to the island had wanted to shop

in the boutiques or hang out at all the in places. The popular beaches and the buzzy bars. And that had been fine because he enjoyed that too.

Or he had, anyway.

Until Tiffany's delight in the backstreets, in their riot of colour and their clashing contrasts between old and new, had made him see it through fresh eyes again. And the way she'd smiled at the locals who had greeted him, and been so utterly at home in his favourite little local taverna, had cemented the feeling that she *got* him.

Understood him in a way that no other woman had. Him. Plain old Theo.

Not Theo Callisthenes, the billionaire. Not Theo Callisthenes, the CEO. Not Theo Callisthenes, the playboy with the black Amex and the superyacht.

Theo, the kid who had grown up listening to old Greek men spinning tales of mermaids. Theo, the teenager who had fucked up and hurt one of his closest friends. Theo, the uni student who'd been attacked by an old lady with a frilly pink umbrella. Theo, the man who loved his family so deeply he liked being surrounded by framed reminders.

And that was big. And new.

She'd said last night that she'd been swept away in the fantasy of it all, and he'd admitted he had been too, and the fact they'd both been feeling the same thing had been the straw that broke the camel's back as far as the dare had been concerned. What had started as a physical need for her had become, in that moment, something else.

Something bigger. Something she hadn't been able to explain. But he'd felt it too. That moment hadn't been about sex, it had been about connecting.

With Tiffany.

And that drove him from the bed because he didn't know the first thing about connecting with just one woman. Spending time with just one woman.

But he knew he wanted to.

* * *

Ten minutes later, Theo was stepping onto the terrace where Tiffany was still at the railing admiring the vista. He passed the table and flashes of last night replayed in his head. The table, the shower, his bed, the pool. Then back to his bed before their hunger had been slaked and exhaustion had dragged them into a deep slumber.

He didn't know how he could want her again so soon and so urgently – but he did. It was more than that though; the desire to see her on his terrace was just as urgent. Summoning all his willpower, he slipped in beside her – not behind.

'You look like you belong here,' he murmured.

Because it was the truth. He'd thought that yesterday as he'd watched her tapping away on her keyboard, pausing occasionally to stare at the sea. And last night as she'd eaten spanakopita and laughed at his jokes. And definitely right now, standing barefoot in yesterday's dress staring at the view as if trying to commit it to memory.

She startled a little and he wasn't sure if it was because she hadn't heard him approach or because his words had discomforted her.

Quickly recovering her poise, she smiled at him before grabbing his hand, unfurling his fingers and placing the opal and diamond ring in his palm.

'Thank you, Theo,' she said as she curled his fingers over it.

'For everything. For all of this.' She gestured to the view and villa. 'And for Mikey.'

Theo frowned, alarm spiking his pulse. Why did this sound like goodbye? 'Are you... leaving?'

She nodded. 'I think it's best.'

What? Wait... No. 'Because of last night?'

'Uh huh. And the day before that. It's been amazing but it is all a fantasy, and I thought I'd be okay going back below deck, but after all this' – she gestured to the view – 'I think it'll just be too weird. And I think the rest of the crew will pick up on the vibe and it'll be weird for them, too. I know I still have a month left on my contract but—'

Theo, his brain grappling with this surprise turn of events, interrupted with a dismissive wave of his hand. 'Don't worry about it.'

'Thanks.'

Thanks? She seemed so... calm while a deep pit of what the fuck tore wide open inside him. 'Where will you go?' Which wasn't what he wanted to ask but seemed the most obvious thing in the situation.

'I'm not sure. I want to finish my book so I'll probably look at some long-term housesitting gigs. I joined an agency after I left Ōceanós.'

'No.' He shook his head. 'You should stay here.'

The offer was out before Theo had fully thought it through, but it made perfect sense. The villa wasn't used a lot of the year and would be even less so as summer wound down, and she wouldn't be gone from his life. They'd have time to figure things out.

'Theo... no.' She shook her head. 'Thank you though.'

'Gratis,' he hastily assured her in case she thought he was after rent.

She laughed again. 'It's not that. It's just…'

Just what? She clearly adored it here. 'Why not?' he pressed. 'You said yourself it's inspirational.'

'And, quite coincidentally, very convenient to you.'

Yes. That was very much the point as far as he was concerned. A smiled curved his mouth. 'Would that be so bad?'

'Theo.' She sighed. 'Yes.'

'Why?'

'Because you and I can't do that.'

'Or maybe,' he suggested tentatively, 'we can?' Okay, yes, it appeared that he was contemplating having his first ever *not* one-and-done thing but, it turned out, when Tiffany was the woman, it didn't feel so scary.

Not that she appeared to agree as she looked at him aghast before she pushed away from the railing muttering, 'No, no, no. This can't be happening.' Which obviously was not a good sign…

With a cold lump of dread in his stomach, Theo turned to watch her pace a few steps before turning back to face him, her arms folded across her waist like armour.

'You only think you want this because it's a novelty to you. But it's not just us and our hearts—'

She stopped abruptly, like she hadn't meant to say the word *heart* but it was too late – Theo had heard it. Did that mean she was feeling more, too?

'We have others to think of,' she continued, clearly deciding that barrelling right on would negate what she'd said. 'Because when whatever you think this is ends, which it will because you'll get tired of being with one woman all the time and I have trust issues with men who can't keep it in their pants, your brother and my friend will be forced to take sides, which might very well cause them some difficulties. They'll have to pick and choose who they invite to what places and which events, like

their baby's christening and birthday parties, and they'll probably argue about which one of us is going to be the godparent.
Your family would probably feel the need to take sides as well
and I'm betting it won't be Kelsey's. And we'll be responsible for
an entire family feud.'

Theo blinked at the mishmash of worst-case scenarios and
diabolical conclusions delivered in an increasingly strident tone.
She was breathing a little hard after her word vomit, which
made him wonder how long she'd been stewing on this crap.

'Okay.' He nodded calmly because she was quite worked up,
as though even the thought of something happening between
them had her running scared. 'But what if none of those things
happens and we just don't put any pressure on ourselves and
just roll the dice? See how it evolves?'

That was how people did this couple thing, right?

She shook her head vehemently. 'I can't see how things
evolve with you. Look at you.' She flapped a hand up and down
in his direction. 'You're gorgeous and filthy rich and we have
amazing sex and you live in this place that just blows my mind.
And it would be way too easy to get in over my head.'

Theo hadn't ever thought being wealthy would be a negative
with a woman, but his gut was telling him it wasn't his money, it
was the getting in over her head that was making her skittish.

'But you're thirty-five,' she continued, 'and never been in a
relationship your entire life. And I've had my fair share of one-
night stands too, Theo, so I have no issue with them, but when
I'm rolling the dice with a guy, I need to know he knows how to
do that. My father couldn't keep it in his pants but at least my
mother hadn't known that before she committed to him. What
kind of fool would I be knowing about it and walking into it
anyway?'

Well... fuck. There it was. Thanks to her father, Tiffany's

trust in men was permanently dented and she was protecting herself from the kind of emotional turmoil she'd endured as a teenager. Risking her heart must be a huge leap of faith, especially on a guy who'd never committed to any woman.

He couldn't blame her for having doubts about him, but to be judged on her father's past behaviours seemed particularly unfair. But then when was life fair?

Her phone rang. 'Don't answer it,' he pleaded. If they could just hash this out, he was sure he'd be able to talk her off the ledge.

'It's Mikey's ring tone,' she said, stalking to the table and snatching it up. 'Hey, Mikey,' she said with forced brightness as she headed for the railing.

'Mikey? Mikey!' She frowned as she came to a halt. 'Slow down, I can't understand what you're saying.'

Alarmed, Theo took a couple of steps towards her as she said, 'What? What about Dad? Is he hurt? Did he get bucked?'

A hot prickle slid down Theo's spine as he watched a cloud of confusion on Tiffany's face change into something else as the colour drained from her cheeks.

'What do you mean, he's dead?' Fingers covered her mouth as she glanced at Theo, her eyes wide. 'But... how?' She listened then and didn't say much, just nodded a couple of times before saying, 'I'll get there as soon as I can,' and hung up.

She stared at her phone for a beat or two, as though she was having trouble remembering how it had got there, before she looked at him. She was ghostly pale and her fingers were trembling as Theo stepped closer only to have her shake her head and ward him back with her hand.

Steeling himself against her rejection, he said, 'What do you need?'

'I have to go home.'

He nodded briskly. 'Give me ten minutes, I'll arrange it.'

22

ONE MONTH LATER...

Tiffany sat on the screened back porch of the homestead, a glass of her father's best whisky in hand. She'd come to escape the mill of people who were gathered in the large area of manicured lawn to the front for her father's wake. With the autopsy requirements and the extra challenges of getting his body back to Balmain Downs from Sydney where he'd been at the time of his heart attack – including some minor flooding from early rains – there'd been quite the delay with the funeral.

And now it was done and he'd been laid to rest at the small cemetery in town, she felt like she could breathe again and maybe come to terms with the fact that she'd never come to terms with their estrangement. She'd have thought that their schism would make his eventual death easier. After all, she'd already spent years grieving the loss of the man she'd thought he was.

But it turned out estrangement only made the grief worse. Because guilt was thrown into the mix. Guilt at never having resolved their issues, or at least saying all the things that twelve-year-old Tiffany hadn't been able to articulate. Guilt at never even trying to forgive or understand and perhaps move on.

What her father had done had cut her to the core, but listening to the eulogy in the funeral, she realised that, to others, he was more than his worst impulses. That he was well regarded and respected. That he would be missed. And that ultimately, he was just a man, as fallible and flawed as the next one, and that she should never have hero-worshipped him in the first place because no person could live up to that.

She wasn't sure if she'd ever forgive him for the emotional blackmail, but being home again, amongst friends and family and landscapes that were part of her DNA and talking to people who knew him differently, had helped her see him differently and perhaps let go a little bit.

Sighing, she took a slug of the whiskey, her gaze falling on the open laptop sitting on the low rickety table in front of her. Blurry pictures of Theo on his superyacht sunbaking next to some random woman on a boat filled the screen. It hurt – more than she cared to analyse – to see them, but she was hardly surprised.

Deep down she'd expected it.

Theo had reverted to type and if it helped draw a line through the feelings that had only grown fonder with his absence, then that was surely a good thing.

He'd called and texted regularly the past month. Had even wanted to come to the funeral, especially as Kelsey hadn't been able to make it because her blood pressure was up and the doctor had advised against flying long distance. But Tiffany had asked him not to. She was working through enough complicated emotions without adding her nagging feelings for Theo into the mix.

'Hey.'

Tiffany turned to find Mikey strolling her way, and she closed the laptop as he sat in the wicker chair next to hers. 'How's it going out there?' she asked as they tapped tumblers.

'Bear is telling tales of the old days,' he said with a smile.

She laughed. It had been a shock to see him turn up at the church. He'd been old as dirt when she'd been a kid and Tiffany had assumed he'd passed away years ago.

'I forgot to tell you,' Mikey said as he stared into his glass, 'that Dad told me to tell you he was sorry.'

Tiffany's head swivelled to stare at her brother. 'What?'

The past month had been a blur and they hadn't really spoken about anything, not even the news about Mikey's upcoming European tour. He'd just told her that their father had tuned up out of the blue to see him at the gallery, even buying the not-for-sale painting of Balmain Downs, and then had collapsed clutching his chest.

Mikey nodded as he looked at her. 'He was lying on the gallery floor looking terrible. Grey and sweaty, and we were waiting for the ambulance. I could hear it screaming nearer and nearer and he was grunting and I was fucking shitting myself that he was going to die and telling him to hang on, hang on, and then he just looked at me and said, "Tell Tiff I'm sorry," and then he slumped down and stopped breathing and the paramedics couldn't revive him.'

She blinked. She didn't know what to say to that. Her father had never said sorry for putting her in the middle like he had.

'I'm really sorry, it slipped my mind. It's been so crazy and it was a pretty intense incident, and I feel like I've barely seen you since you got back.'

'It's fine.' She had flown direct to Darwin and Mikey had

stayed in Sydney until a few days ago, so there was that. Plus she could only imagine how traumatic it must have been for him to watch complete strangers trying to revive their dead father right in front of him.

'Does it help?' he asked.

'I... don't know.'

It was a startling revelation, and Tiffany wished he'd been able to tell her before he died, but the fact they were his last words perhaps hinted that at least his actions back then had weighed on his mind.

She shrugged. 'Maybe it will... eventually.'

'Better than the combination to the safe.'

Tiffany hooted out a laugh at the running family joke about her father's secrecy around the safe, and he joined her, which was how their mother found them moments later. 'Mikey, someone called Rusty is asking for you,' she said.

'Ooh.' Mikey grinned. 'I think I've possibly found the only gay man in a thousand kilometres radius.'

'Eww,' Tiffany teased. 'Cracking on at a funeral. Classy.'

'Beggars can't be choosers out here.'

He left with a swagger in his step and Tiffany shook her head as the door shut behind him. Even though she and Mikey Face-Timed often and texted all the time, she'd missed him terribly.

Her mother took Mikey's chair and Tiffany braced herself for whatever conversation was to follow. She'd seen her mum almost every day since she'd been home, but their interactions had been stilted and inane.

'It was a big turn out,' Tiffany said, not comfortable enough in her mother's company to let silence build.

'Yes.'

She'd expected her mother to have some kind of dig about how many of the female mourners her ex-husband had bonked

– sarcastic verbal asides had been her go-to since their divorce – but she didn't, and Tiffany wondered if maybe her mother was also facing a bit of a reckoning.

They chatted about frivolous topics until her mother decided to get real. 'What are your plans now the funeral is over?'

'I... don't know.' Tiffany had put her writing plans aside for the past month and she wanted to get back to it, but she felt a little in limbo at the moment.

It made sense to stay here and complete the book, but the red dirt and gum trees were so at odds to the world of blues that made up the Aegean where her mermaids had taken true form and shape, she didn't know if she'd even be able to write here.

'Why don't you stay? I saw you out on Maximillian the other day. You looked like you've never been away.'

Tiffany smiled. Riding her old horse had felt very natural despite not having ridden in almost ten years. And she'd loved the smell of the dust as it was kicked up and the heavy aroma of eucalyptus in the air.

'You've missed it, I can tell.'

'I have,' Tiffany admitted. But it felt more like nostalgia than real actual yearning.

'I'd like it if you stayed.'

Her mother shifted in her chair, her bleached-blonde bob razor-sharp as she plucked imaginary lint off her chic black-and-white checked skirt before meeting Tiffany's eye.

'I'd like the chance to apologise and make up to you for how I blamed you all those years ago. I was so angry at your father and the fact you knew what a fool he'd made of me made me feel so stupid. It was easier to take it out on you than face the fact that the man I loved had been serially unfaithful to me. But' – she reached across and patted Tiffany's arm – 'it wasn't your fault. And you were a child and it was just... unforgiveable of me.'

It wasn't your fault.

Well... how about that. *Two* apologies in one day. Obviously, Marshall Wainwright's death had made her mother examine her role in the breakdown of their marriage. Maybe even made her realise life was short and death was very, very final.

'Yeah, it was,' Tiffany agreed. 'Just not sure why it's taken you so long.' Her father's death might have made Tiffany more open to forgiveness, but it also made her more open to ask the hard questions she'd been avoiding all these years.

Her mother shifted uncomfortably. 'You've been gone for ten years, sweetheart.'

'You could have picked up the phone.' *You could have said sorry the next day. Or the day after. Or the day after that.*

Swallowing hard, her mother blinked back tears. 'You're right. I'm sorry for that, too.'

Tiffany nodded slowly, her old anger not as important right now as her mother's obvious remorse. And perhaps they could work on mending those bridges.

If she stayed.

'Beverly? There you are.' A woman Tiffany didn't recognise popped her head out the door that led from the internal hallway onto the porch. 'Marjorie's leaving and was looking for you.'

'I'm coming,' she said, straightening her skirt. The other woman departed and her mother stood. 'Will you think about it?' she asked.

Tiffany nodded. 'Yeah. I will.' And she would.

Tiffany's phone rang as the tippy tap of her mother's heels receded. *Theo.* She shut her eyes and almost let it go to voicemail. Those photos on her laptop told her she should, but the masochist in her needed to hear his voice today.

'Hey,' she said, injecting some cheer into her voice.

'Hey.' His voice was exactly what she needed, rich and low, the burr of his soft accent rubbing against her skin as if he was sitting beside her. 'How did it go?'

Tiffany filled him on the details and they laughed about Bear showing up, and she told him about the twin apologies, and it felt so good to talk to him she just wanted to cry. And she hadn't cried since she'd stepped off the plane in Darwin.

'My mother wants me to stay home for a bit,' she blurted out as he was telling her about a painting he'd seen of a mermaid in an art gallery in Athens.

There was a long pause on his end. 'Okay... how do you feel about that?'

Like she wanted him to want her to *not* stay. Even if he was back to his playboy ways. Which made zero fucking sense. But hey, she'd just buried her estranged father and found out about his apology as well as getting another from her mother.

It was a day for emotional whiplash.

'It means something that she asked.'

'Yes.'

'And this place.' She stared out at the red roof of the tractor shed beyond the green fringe of lawn and caught the faint whiff of cow manure that was a constant out here. 'It's as much a part of me as Mykonos is of you.'

'You've missed it?'

It did still call to her and she knew if she stayed that she'd probably slip back into the way of things out here. But life on a cattle station was all-consuming – a hard daily grind ruled by the elements and stock prices, neither of which they could control. And would she pursue her dream of finishing her book if she stayed here or give up because there was just too much to do around the place?

'Some of it,' she murmured.

'Well, if it helps, I'm missing you.'

Tiffany shut her eyes as her heart gave a little lurch. No, it didn't help. Why couldn't he just let her go? He'd obviously moved on. 'Really, Theo?' She gave a laugh so dry it almost grazed her throat. 'I know we're at the ass end of Earth here,' she said derisively, 'but the internet does reach Australia.'

Another pause. 'What's that supposed to mean?'

She rolled her eyes as she reached across and lifted the lid on her laptop. 'The pictures, Theo. You. And a woman? On your yacht.'

He said something in Greek she was pretty sure was a swear word. 'Hold, please.'

Tiffany blinked at his command as she stared at the pictures. It had been another stunning day wherever they were, and her heart ached at the way Theo was laughing at the mystery woman.

'Tiffany, that is not what it looks like,' he said after about thirty seconds. 'That is Deidre, for Christ sakes.'

What? Grabbing her laptop, Tiffany pulled it closer. The images were blurry so she supposed it could be Deidre, now she looked more closely.

'Fucking paparazzi,' he muttered. 'I bet if you saw the full frames of those photos you'd see Vasilis and the girls off to the side. Please believe me.'

For what it was worth, she did believe him. But this was always going to be the problem being with Theo. Pictures being snapped of him that could easily be misrepresented. Was she strong enough for that?

She wasn't right now.

'I've not been with anyone since you left. Damn it, I don't want anyone else. You're completely under my skin. I can't stop thinking about you. The first thing I think about when I wake up is calling you because I want to hear your voice and I hate that you're on the other side of the world and going through this all alone.'

Tiffany sucked in a breath at the anguish in his voice and at the revelation. She knew Theo had to be completely outside his comfort zone, and her pulse fluttered madly over what it might mean. Was he telling her he had feelings for her?

But, if so, why not just come out and say it?

Because even with her father's apology out there, it didn't undo the mistrust he'd sown in her life. That didn't just disappear because the man who had been responsible was now in the ground.

Trust lost was always the hardest to regain.

So maybe what she most needed now – particularly now – was time and space to work through those things and rid herself of that inner wariness that kept her from being able to let her heart out of its cage and have faith that it wouldn't be betrayed.

And maybe he needed time to figure out exactly what he meant by not wanting anyone else. And if he was really sure.

'You know what, Theo. I think my mother's right. Staying here for a while is probably just what I need right now. I think I need some space to work through a bunch of stuff I've never really worked through. And maybe you need some space to be sure, too.'

'Tiffany, I am—'

'Please, Theo,' she interrupted, not wanting to hear him say 'sure', especially if he was mistaking missing her for something else. 'Can we just take some time?'

A long silence followed, and she could picture him gripping his phone and glaring into space. Theo Callisthenes was not a man who liked to wait. But he had already – for her. So maybe he could wait a little longer?

'Of course,' he murmured eventually, his voice soft. 'Take all the time you need.'

'Thank you, Theo.' She pronounced it with its full Greek inflection and ended the call.

23

FOUR WEEKS LATER...

Theo stood on the terrace squinting against the vicious sparkle of morning sun on the Aegean. Even though it was November and the days were cooler, the sea was still a blinding blue. As blindingly blue as the building behind was blindingly white and the bougainvillea creeping over the facade was blindingly purple.

It was stunningly, blindingly perfect. Except he hated it. Because he was here and Tiffany was in fucking Australia.

He'd gone into work this morning and lasted for two hours before his brain had churned with thoughts of Tiffany, rendering him utterly useless, so he'd jumped in the company helicopter and been standing on the terrace of his villa forty minutes later, his tie and jacket discarded. Because this was where he felt closest to her.

Please, Theo, can we just take some time?

But how long was that? Was it weeks? Because it had been four already. Or was it months? Theo had never been a particularly patient man and, as she had pointed out, relationships weren't his forte, but he knew enough about her to know that she was going through a lot and he was going to have to wait till she figured it out.

He smashed his hand on the railing. Fuck. Fuck. *Fuuuuck!*

'Here you are.'

Theo turned to find Ari striding towards him in his business suit. He must have caught the helicopter straight back once it had landed on the pad on top of their building.

'Go away, Ari.'

His brother grinned, unconcerned by Theo's scowl. 'And miss out on seeing you brought to your knees by a woman?'

Ari had told him once, on this very terrace, that one day a woman was going to bring him to his knees and that he hoped he was around to see it.

And here they were.

'Don't worry. I brought the reports with me to read.'

'I don't give a fuck about the reports.' Ari glared at him as he drew level at the railing. 'I want to know what the hell's going on with you.'

'I'm giving her space,' he growled. There was no point pretending it was anything else other than Tiffany making him lose his mind.

'Why?' he demanded.

Theo ground his back molars. 'Because she asked me to.'

'I mean,' Ari said with a sigh, 'why are you indulging her like this? Anything else you wanted, you'd go at it like a bull at a gate.'

'Because she's not some business deal.'

'And?'

'She's just lost her father?'

'And?'

Theo frowned. 'And... she's going through some stuff.'

'*Thee mou!*' Ari muttered. 'But why her?'

'Because I don't want to be with anyone else.'

Ari sighed again and pinched the bridge of his nose as if he was holding on to his last shred of patience.

'You know I was standing right here when Pappou challenged me over my feelings for Kelsey so I'm going to do the same thing for you. Are you ready? Maybe,' he said, slowly and purposefully, as though Theo was a little dim, 'the reason you're out of your mind right now and ill-tempered and generally unpleasant to be around is not just because you suddenly don't want to be with anyone else but Tiffany, but because you're in love with her.'

Theo blinked at the announcement. This was love? How could that possibly be true when it felt like he was developing an ulcer?

Anxiety. Concern. Obsession, even...

And yet, looking in his brother's eyes, he could see the truth of it. Could feel the truth of it. He was in love with Tiffany.

'*This* is love?'

'Uh huh.'

'Like... someone's punched me in the gut and I can't breathe?'

'Uh huh.'

'I thought it was supposed to be giddy and fucking... unicorns pooping glitter?'

Ari shrugged. 'Some people get that. Not us.'

'Well, that sucks.'

'Yup,' Ari agreed as he grabbed his brother by the shoulder. 'Now what are you going to do about it?'

'I don't know.' He stared at Ari incredulously. 'I don't know how to do this. You've done it twice. You tell me.'

Bugging his eyes, Ari said, 'Go and tell her.'

Theo bugged his eyes back. 'She asked me to give her space.'

'Yes, but you haven't given her all the information.'

'What if I do that and she tells me she doesn't love me?'

'Then too bad for you. You leave and come back to work.'

God, he hated that option. 'What if she's not sure and wants more space?'

'Then you still leave. But you don't go far and you let her know that you're there for her when she's ready.'

'What if that takes a while?'

'It takes as long as it takes, dumbass. All you need is your laptop and an internet connection and you can run the company from anywhere.'

'You want me to live in the outback?'

'Hey, I lived in a caravan park. For months. You can live in the outback.'

That was true. He was Theo Callisthenes, the CEO of a billion-dollar cruise ship company. He could kick outback ass.

'Okay then.' Mind suddenly made up, he nodded. 'I'm doing it.'

'Atta boy,' Ari said, slapping him on the back then pulling him into a bear hug.

Love might feel like a rupturing peptic ulcer, but if Tiffany loved him back then he'd stock up on anti-aids and take it like a man.

* * *

Three days later, Tiffany was in the stables rubbing down Maximillian and chatting to her mother, who was rubbing down her horse, Moonshine. They'd been out riding all morning, helping with fences, and she was looking forward to a long, cool drink of the Pimm's and lemonade her mother had made up in a jug in the fridge.

They'd talked a lot the last month, her mother coming over most days, and although things would probably never be the way they were, they were better, and she was happy for that. Tiffany didn't want to still feel angry with her mother till the day she died, not when that had been such a punch to her gut with her dad.

And knowing how painful it had felt seeing Theo in those paparazzi pictures a month ago, she had a little more insight into how gutting her father's betrayal had been for her mother.

'Tiffany?'

Freezing mid-brush with the curry comb, Tiffany blinked. Had she just conjured Theo up by merely thinking about him? Turning slowly, she saw a figure silhouetted against the backdrop of bright blue sky. A very familiar figure, tall and broad, in blue jeans – a first – boots and a button-down shirt.

'Theo?'

'*Yassas*, Tiffany,' he said as he stepped inside and came closer.

It was him, and *gah*, he was a sight for sore eyes. She'd asked him to give her space and he had, but as a hot rush of emotion she knew without a shadow of a doubt was love flooded through her system, she realised she'd been such an idiot.

She been ignoring her feelings whilst she worked on her other emotions around her father and the unresolved stuff from her childhood and had figured somewhere deep down that Theo would tire of the wait and move on.

But seeing him again, she was so relieved he was here she almost sobbed.

Love for him poured from her chest as the truth rang clear as a bell. She, Tiffany Wainwright, was in love with Theo Callisthenes. And she had no idea how that was going to work; she just knew she wasn't scared any more to feel it and that she was going to give it a red-hot try – if it was reciprocated.

She ran at him then, dusty jeans and shirt and smelling like horse, her heart suddenly flying as she threw herself into his arms and kissed him with all the pent-up emotion that had built over the weeks they'd been apart. Taking it as a good sign that he wasn't stopping her – in fact, he was enthusiastically partaking in their lip lock – Tiffany wanted to drag him to the ground and kiss him some more and demand that he love her back.

She would have, too, had her mother's amused 'Tiff?' not brought her up short.

They broke apart then as if they'd been zapped by a cattle prod, but her hand still clung to his sleeve because she didn't want to let him go, and also, she was a little too dizzy to stand unaided.

'Mum,' she said, feeling very much like they were teenagers who had been caught making out. 'This is Theo.' In normal introductions it would be usual for her to explain the nature of their relationship, but Tiffany figured her mother had already worked that one out. 'Theo, this is my mother, Beverly Martin.'

Thankfully, her mother was walking forward and extending her hand to him, so Tiffany didn't have to test the solidity of her legs. 'So, you're the one my daughter has been mooning over,' she said with a smile as they shook hands.

Tiffany bugged her eyes at her mother. 'I have not been mooning.'

'Maybe not.' She winked at Theo. 'But a mother knows when something is up.' She beamed at both of them. 'Come inside when you're ready, I have a nice cool jug of something prepared.'

She left them alone then and Theo promptly gathered her back in his arms, but he evaded her mouth as she stood on tippy toe. 'Wait,' he said with a smile. 'I need to tell you something first.'

Tiffany sighed. 'Okay, fine,' she teased.

'I know you wanted space and if you need more, then I'll go but not without telling you that I love you.'

'Oh, thank God.' Tiffany's forehead pressed to his chest, and she gripped the front of his shirt standing in his embrace, absorbing those three little words for long moments.

'I'm sorry,' he said, his lips pressing into the top of her head. 'I didn't know how much space was too much space, or even if what I was feeling was love. I knew I couldn't stop thinking about you and didn't want to be with anyone else, and Ari had to explain to me that feeling like I'd been sucker punched and brewing an ulcer were classic symptoms of love and I was suffering them big time.'

Circling her arms around his waist, Tiffany laughed as she tipped her chin back to look into his strong face. His whiskers were longer than she was used to, which would have probably looked haggard on anyone else but just added to his charisma.

'If it helps, I've been feeling pretty sucker punched too.'

'Really?'

'Really.'

A huge smile spread across his mouth. 'Is that because you love me too?'

Tiffany nodded. 'It is.'

He laughed then, picking her up and twirling her around because apparently she wasn't giddy enough. 'Why do people do this?' he asked, smiling down at her.

'Because it's the best worst feeling in the world.'

'Oh God.' He blinked. 'You're right.'

She shrugged. 'Of course I am. Now can I kiss you?'

'Not yet, there's more.'

'Okay.' Tiffany braced herself for how ominous that sounded.

'I need you to know that I understand you're going through a lot at the moment and if you need to stay here, then we'll stay. Hell, I'll move here if that's what you need. And the paparazzi thing? I'm afraid it's part of my life, but I suspect when they know I'm now a one-woman man, I'll be far too boring for them and they'll leave us alone. But you have to trust me that all of my wild oats have been sown and you are the only woman for me, and I know that's not an easy ask for you because of your dad, but I promise I'm going to work every day to make sure you're secure in my fidelity. Then there's kids.'

Tiffany smiled. He wasn't joking about there being more.

'I know you said you weren't sure about kids but, to be honest, the thought of having babies with you makes me kinda giddy – in a good way,' he assured her. 'So I'm happy to get reversal; just say the word.'

Tiffany smiled. He was just too damn sweet, this badass billionaire of hers. 'I don't know about kids but I love that it's not a hard line for you any more, so let's cross that bridge when we get to it, yes?'

He nodded. 'Yes.'

'And I understand about the paparazzi and how tabloids can misrepresent things. I'm not saying it won't be challenging at times, but I do trust you.' She did. Not every man was her father. There were plenty of honourable men out there in the world; she only had to look to Theo's family for confirmation. 'And I promise to work every day to show you that.'

'Good idea,' he said with a smile. 'We'll both promise.'

'Lastly, I don't need to stay here. It's the place I grew up and I never thought I'd leave, and I do love it, but life has taught me that home is where the person you love is. I'd like to come back to Balmain Downs more often than I have because my mum and I are working things out and I'd like to keep going with that, but it's not my home any more.'

'We'll come back as often as you want.' He lifted a hand and tucked a loose tendril that had fallen from her ponytail behind her ear.

We'll. Tiffany's heart skipped a beat and she smiled – she liked the sound of that.

'What I'd really like is to live on Mykonos. If that's possible? In the villa. It's close to Athens and Kelsey and, ohhh, Theo! I can write there. I could spend my life writing there. I mean... it's so crazy to comprehend that a villa on Mykonos is my life now.'

Tiffany didn't even know what to do with the whole billionaire thing yet.

'Believe it,' he murmured. 'Because you deserve the best. And I can't wait for Mykonos to be as much a part of your life as it is mine.'

That sounded pretty damn good to Tiffany. 'Now can I kiss you?'

He grinned. 'For as long as you want.'

Tiffany didn't need any further invitation...

EPILOGUE
TWO YEARS LATER...

It was another blindingly blue day as the champagne flowed on the sundeck of the *Nerida*, which was anchored just off Mykonos, basking in the Aegean sun. A small party of elegantly dressed people were there to toast the release of *A Mermaid Moon*, the first book in the Astraon trilogy, which had been sold for a high six-figure sum at auction a year ago. There was to be a huge publisher launch party in London next week, but it was this party Tiffany had looked forward to the most.

Just like their wedding, it was a small affair, with only a handful of her and Theo's closest friends and family. Theo's parents and grandparents plus Tiffany's mother and Mikey, who'd moved to Paris a year ago. Vasilis and Deidre and the twins were here, as were Dimitri and Helena Kouris. Also present were Ivan – looking resplendent in his kilt – and Kelly, who still claimed they'd known from day one that she and Theo were going to end up together.

And Ari and Kelsey, of course, along with Cora, their now eighteen-month-old little girl who was the apple of everyone's eye.

Tiffany inhaled deeply as she watched the scene from the back railing, a pile of her books ready to be signed nearby. Sunshine warmed her lungs and burst through her chest in a bloom of radiant contentment. Never in a million years had she imagined she could have this kind of life – the man of her dreams, the place of her dreams, the job of her dreams.

'Your soda water,' Theo murmured as he slid in behind her, pulling her back into him, his arms slipping around her waist, his hands splaying against the bulge of her thirty-week baby bump.

'Thank you.'

Kissing her temple, he whispered, 'You did it.'

Tiffany smiled. 'We did it.' Because she couldn't have done it without his faith and encouragement and total belief in her ability.

'Happy?'

'More than I'd ever thought possible. You?'

'I am the luckiest man on the planet.'

She held up her glass. 'To the best worst feeling in the world.'

Chuckling, Theo also raised his glass. 'To love.'

And they tapped.

* * *

MORE FROM AMY ANDREWS

Another book from Amy Andrews, *Undercover Billionaire*, is available to order now here:

https://mybook.to/UndercoverAmyBackAd

ACKNOWLEDGEMENTS

It's been a delight finally giving Theo his HEA. When he appeared in all his cocky, swaggering glory in Ari and Kelsey's story I knew I had to bring him to his knees somehow and when Tiffany also flew from my fingers in that book, I knew I'd found the woman to do it.

Big thanks to Megan Haslam and Boldwood Books for being my conduit to Theo and Tiffany's HEA. In fact, big thanks to everyone at Boldwood. The team is amazing and it's a privilege to be part of their stable of authors.

Thanks also to my agent, Jill Marsal.

As ever, extra special thanks to my readers. It never gets old holding your own book in your hands and it's because of you guys, I get to do that.

Big love xxx